ADV

Judith Day's *Glowin*
of creative writing ar.
psychotherapy. Reading it, I kept imagining psychotherapists in training diving into it—I'd love to teach that class. But here's hoping it is widely read by all. It will be a compelling read for everyone.

—Todd Dean, MD, psychiatrist and psychoanalyst

Beautiful and wise, *Glowing in the Dark* offers a triptych of compelling and complex psychological dramas. Judith Day writes with sorely-needed empathy, in prose graceful and precise. Her characters reveal lives that are heartbreaking, brutal, erotic, and ultimately affirming. A late debut, but well worth the wait!

—John Henry Fleming, author of *Songs for the Deaf* and Professor of Creative Writing at the University of South Florida

Glowing in the Dark is the perfect title for this collection of stories, which are deep, clear-eyed visions of our interconnected souls' dark places as well as their light ones. The compassion glows. The prose glows.

—Arlene Bernstein, psychotherapist and author of *Growing Season: Life Lessons from the Garden*

"I am devoted to dwelling in the present, not the past or future. But the past is devoted to dwelling in me, in hideous ways ...," from Judith Day's "Sit Beside Me," the first of three deeply challenging stories in this, her first collection. Her characters, like the author herself, are unflinching in their pursuit of truth and beauty, love and meaning. Like Mahakala, the bodhisattva of compassion, Judith wields a sharp blade. Perhaps there is no healing without wounding, and no seeing oneself without risking seeing others in all their misery and grace. It's a beautiful book and I'm already looking forward to her next.

—Daniel Coshnear, author of *Separation Anxiety*

In Judith Day's story, "Birthday Present," a woman remembers an assault as "inviting me to go someplace I needed to go." In this collection of a novella and two stories, where people need to go is where trauma and therapy both take us—into the territory of Hades: the underground kingdom, the land of the dead, which Persephone famously enters via rape, Odysseus journeys in order to get home, and Orpheus to rescue his beloved. The land of the dead in Greek mythology is full of voices, stories, and desire: it is the personal and collective unconscious, the quick- change land of dreams, the place where longing and memory wait until the artist or the healer brings light and fashions something we can understand in our waking lives.

Glowing in the Dark is fascinated with the work that is done when necessity presses against a receptive mind, one that can navigate the darkness and make meaning out of suffering. Contrary to contemporary platitudes, such meaning is neither predictable nor obvious; each person does it differently and receives the rewards differently. The point of art and therapy is transformation, but with any real transformation, you can never be sure when it starts or where it ends, or if the wisdom was worth what it cost.

Day's stories are always surprising and can be uncomfortable. They make you want to talk back. They will also make you want to read them again, to glean the knowledge between the lines. Alan, a suicidal psychiatric patient—one of many characters you have met nowhere else—collects autumn leaves by the river. "I thought words might be written on them, but there weren't any. Then I thought if I laid them down in order, the words might turn up." They don't, not for Alan, nor for his psychiatrist, Tim. But for the reader, the words glow.
        —Margaret Diehl, author of *The Boy on the Green Bicycle*

GLOWING
~ IN THE ~
DARK

Stories of Wounded Healers

JUDITH DAY

Glowing in the Dark

A different version of "The Embrace" first appeared in Bottomfish, Vol. 19,
Spring 1998, published by DeAnza College.

Printed in the United States of America

First Printing, 2023

Cover and book design by Asya Blue Design
Cover photo by Judith Day
Author photo by Doug Wheatley

ISBN 978-1-9410666-1-4
Library of Congress Control Number: 2023941239

Wordrunner Press
Petaluma, California
www.wordrunner.com

TABLE OF CONTENTS

For my wounded healers:

Jay Matejcik
Robert K. Hall
Thomas Pope
Ernestine Ward

"Who can take away suffering without entering it?"
—Henri J. M. Nouwen, *The Wounded Healer*

PREFACE

Healers know wounding. This book brings the reader into the lives of a few such people. With their suffering and through their suffering, they are led into personal, exceptional ways of helping others and themselves.

The first story, *Sit Beside Me*, was originally called *Suicide Notes*. It evolved over twenty painful, gratifying years. It is an unconventional tale of the classic wounded healer: a psychiatrist entering his own brokenness while entering the brokenness of a patient, helping them both.

In the second story, *Birthday Present*, a physician and her assailant find healing for themselves and each other during an actual event of wounding. It's erotic, and it is a disturbing story to some people. Originally called *Butterflies*, it emerged over thirty years of multiple re-writings. The story and I have worked on each other, with feedback from other wounded writers. It's a wounded healer of a story.

The third story, *The Embrace*, tells of two wounded psychotherapists tangled in a healing relationship as one of them dies. It was always named *The Embrace*, and an earlier version was published in 1998. The journal that printed it was called *Bottomfish*, which always made me laugh. That journal disappeared and was subsequently reborn as *Red Wheelbarrow*.

Who is the healer? Who is the one healed? I offer this book in the hope that it may reflect, nourish, and honor the real experience of all of us, all people, as helpers.

Judith Day
Monte Rio, California
July 2023

SIT BESIDE ME

Dear _____

Today I thought the man in the doughnut shop could see dead children in my eyes. I had been crying. He took my order—twelve holes, six chocolate and six glazed—and bagged them and rang me up, and he kept glancing at me, searching: what is it about this face that is strange? My just-cried face. I looked back at him. His own face was crooked, and he was comically muscular for a doughnut server. He was not a young man, but he was innocent. He wanted nothing from me.

But I wanted so much from him because I can't fix it. Need somebody else to do it for me.

You reading this (whoever you are) are thinking, *oh yeah we all want somebody to take care of us. Yeah, sure, I'd like to have somebody too, pay my bills and feed me and wipe my ass. But that's not how it is. Grow up and take care of yourself asshole baby. You have to go and kill your-self yeah make a big scene baby sure we'd all like somebody to take endless boundless total care of us, but we don't all go around killing ourselves over it baby baby baby crybaby—*

That's a lot of hate. So tonight, two in the morning, I'm trying to write it away. It doesn't go away. I look inside, put what's there into words, and the words are like that. Well, those words are true but not the whole truth. I'd like to tell you everything, but it's too hard to go on. There is too much hate. It fills my head and slides down to my heart, the hate that says: this is no good. This is bad. The hate happens inside and pushes outside. It happens behind my forehead when I look at things on the table—salt and pepper, magazine, insurance bill, hand. Toy for the cats. All bad. Can't bear it.

Writing a suicide note is not as easy as it sounds. If I could write a good one, I probably wouldn't need to kill myself. But I'm exhausted and I can't get the words right. There are so many of them that need to come out. They tangle up.

This morning my wife, who is always decluttering, pulled a box of old photos from a closet. Beware old photos. These were from my childhood, and one of them, I swear, I had never seen: a family snapshot in someone's yard on a summer day. My great aunt sits in a chair on the right with her legs crossed, barefoot and wearing a stylish cotton dress. In the center of the picture my older brother and sister stand behind another chair, in which my great uncle is lounging. His shirt is open and his hair is rumpled. He is tanned, wet with sweat. His long legs are extended, bare, and spread apart. And I—I am sprawled across my uncle's lap. I am lying across him. Everyone looks at the camera except that I am looking at Uncle Joe's hands, which are folded together on my groin.

I am not a two- or four-year-old, or even six or seven. The date is handwritten on the back of the picture: 1977. I am thirteen years old. My aunt was there, older siblings were there, and it was my mother, I am sure, taking the picture. Nobody saw the boy possessed by the devil.

I tucked the photo in a bookcase and left the house, driving nowhere. I went to the foothills and took a long walk beside a creek, almost a dry bed but with a trickle and occasional pool filled with brown leaves fallen from scrubby willows. Air was fresh, sunshine warm. But the whole time, I was assaulted by thoughts—not good ones. Thoughts are not words in your head. They come with teeth. Teeth on fire. There was a truck parked in a farmyard. The letters painted on the side said "Dead Redeemer." I looked harder and saw reality: "Deck Refinisher."

I must be crazy. I'm a FUBAR: Fucked Up Beyond All Repair. Mental health professionals say that about certain mental patients. When they say it they are smiling, and the smiles say: *I'm not like that. Keep that FUBAR disease away from me.* Medication should help this. It has helped for short periods. But on or off meds—presently off—I always go back to crazy.

I got back in the car and drove around town and saw the doughnut shop. I never eat doughnuts, but I was looking for shelter from myself. After I left the shop with my bag of fried holes and got out to the street, I stuffed a glazed one into my mouth. It seemed to help. I took another two holes with me and set the nearly full bag down on a bench at a bus stop and drove home. When I got there, I took the photo from between the books and carried it upstairs and put it in the drawer of my bedside table.

Sincerely,

Tim

Dear _____

Another suicide note tonight. What's the point? My words are not enough. There is too much hate, and there isn't enough love.

It can be frustrating for other people to deal with a suicidal person. We don't have what you need to help us. We don't have enough good stuff inside. The ego structures. The inner good mommy. For a while in my teenage years, over thirty years ago, I turned to Jesus to fill in the gaps. Jesus was a refuge, and he went a long way toward helping, but he just couldn't get a toehold inside me. No inner structures for Jesus to climb on. Not even a cross inside me.

Your love is there and sometimes I feel it. I'm doing my best to feel it just as you've all done your best to give it. None of us has failed. It's a hard way to live, in relationships like that, but it's not failure. But it's too hard to do forever, without hope of repair. Please don't condemn us, either you or me or somebody else, as failures. I am living the best that I can.

I know how hard it is to get close to somebody like me. But there are people like me who I do get close to. That's because I am a psychiatrist.

Sincerely,

Timothy M. Jones, M.D.

P.S. One thing I know is that placebo heals. Placebo means this: what a person believes in can cure him.

Dear _____,

Last week I stopped going to therapy after six years with Martine. She is as solid, creative, and loving a therapist as anyone could be. I did very good work with her. My self-esteem grew; my ease with my life grew. When my only child moved on in life, away from our home, my simmering discontent about my marriage was unveiled. Working with Martine helped me diminish the power of my fruitless mental picking at whether Dana and I should stay together in our less-than-perfect union. We're here, we love each other, it's simple and true.

Martine helped me with all of this and more, and I will always feel warmhearted and deeply respectful in thinking of her. There was no good reason to stop therapy, but I did. I think I needed to be alone with myself. Some things I'm not ready to talk about with anyone. I don't even know what they are. But if I don't have to talk about them, I might find out. Since stopping therapy, I've hit some deep lows, but I also feel excited and at times a little giddy.

For one thing, not seeing Martine now leaves me freer to move forward with killing myself: to plan, to act. But so far, I refuse to even make a plan. Options roll through my mind like balls I toss for my cats, just that random and insignificant. So I'm not planning it, but I seem to be writing a suicide note. Maybe I'm getting close.

Am I writing my notes to Martine? She is one of the dear people who have helped me live with my pain. Martine helped a lot. My wife, Dana, helps immeasurably, irrefutably, forever and always. The doughnut man helped too. I think the notes are for all of you. Every time you talked to me, that was help. Every time you were kind to me instead of mean: help. Nothing moves me more than knowing how you have truly helped me. Help is good. But I'm looking for something else. There are times when I glimpse it. If I leave myself alone, it might find me.

At this moment I feel compelled to write thank you notes: to my wife, to my daughter, friends, even to strangers. To my patients. To my mother and my father.

But not to my uncle, who is dead anyway. When I die, will he be waiting at the tunnel's end? Tunnel to hell. I could kill him there, over and over, for eternity.

Sincerely,
Tim

Dear_____,

Oh, how I wish you could help me. As soon as I woke this morning, I was at war inside, and I lay in bed with it after Dana got up. Enemy thoughts spray my guts with artillery, leaving craters filled with raging fire. The screaming wounded claw their way out of the pits onto solid ground only to have it crumble away into the next flaming trench. Fragmentation, inner assault, every ground of peace or sanity gained just as quickly falling away. There is no reason for this kind of waking, but it is a frequent start to my day. The vagaries of mood waste no time.

Why do I suffer so? If it's my nature, medication could do the trick. It doesn't, really. It gives respite but is not an enduring release. So, let's look at nurture.

In the womb I was terrorized, I am sure, by my angry, terrified, alcoholic mother. At my birth I refused for long moments to take a breath. In early childhood I went on what the family jokingly called a "hunger strike." But it's really no joke when a preschooler won't eat. I would not eat and visited my first shrink, to whom I would not speak.

At age five I was severely beaten with the buckle end

12

of a belt by my father, who was by far the better of the two parents. He blew his stack at my mother and took it out on me. He never did anything like it again, and we always liked each other. But he was as full of rage as my mother, and they fought wildly. He also talked too much, told me all his troubles, and was afraid to listen to mine. It was so natural for me to become a psychiatrist.

My great uncle, my mother's aunt's husband, sexually molested me from the time I was four years old, maybe earlier, into my teens. He told me not to tell anyone; it was our secret only. It *was* our secret, and I told no one because the child I was knew how special it is to have a secret with an uncle. He was a prominent state government official. A government official molesting a little boy. As far as I know, it was the only dangerous thing he did. He was a careful man who put away his clothes and garden tools with chilling precision. Cutting his meat just so, arranging the potatoes and vegetables. Every morning of his life, the same breakfast of half grapefruit, single poached egg, and thin toast lightly buttered.

He would take me to motels out the highway or to hotels on trips with him. The trips, to an aquarium or a Civil War battleground, were for my pleasure and education. But after we left the fish or the graves, we would go out to dinner where he flirted with me and started the coy touching. The closer he came, the farther away he went. He pushed his face into mine, his eyes glazed over. I went away, too. There was some way I had of not being there, though I don't know where I went. I have been coming back ever since, but part of me is still there.

What was I to him? I don't think he loved me at all. Sometimes, they do. They love, really, and they mix it all up with taking and using. Uncle Joe, I don't think he loved me. He controlled me. He gave me money. Another precursor of my chosen profession—give me money, I'll be nice to you, I'll let you say anything. I'll give you intimacy.

Once, when I was a teenager, he gave me a suede jacket that he picked out for me. We had lunch together at a restaurant near the state capitol, where he was greeted jovially by waiters and colleagues. Then he insisted on taking me shopping and had me try on several pants and shirts before picking out the leather jacket to match my sandy hair. It took a long time because he wasn't sure which length he wanted. In the end, he overruled a full-length coat, in which I felt ridiculous, and picked the jacket. I liked it too, but I never wore it.

I wet the bed until age twelve, set fires, stole money from my mother's purse, and shoplifted. I got hauled to the emergency room with stomach pains that had no diagnosis. I told mostly lies, and I had no friends. In my teens I became promiscuous, with girls. Boys were of no interest to me. When I started driving, I passed cars on hills at high speed. I drank too much, often alone.

Slowly, I learned good things and met good people. I drink moderately now, meditate frequently. I pray. I take time for life's small joys: listening to music, walking in nature, eating vegetables and whole grains. I've walked the Twelve Steps and the Eightfold Noble Path. I live one day at a time. I am devoted to dwelling in the present, not the past or future.

But the past is devoted to dwelling in me, in hideous ways, voracious for my sanity, my soul. I have times of joy, peace, gratitude. These times are dwarfed and consumed by the times of angst. The beast occupies me. And it may be gaining ground.

I think I will kill myself when I can meet certain conditions:

(1) The act must be done without anger or despair. It must be an intelligent, caring act. To relieve my suffering would qualify.

(2) It can only be done when I can write a suicide note with which I am satisfied.

Sincerely,
Tim

⁓

Dear You Who Might Understand,

I have a wife and daughter. How could I kill myself?

I'm married, twenty-three years now, to a fine woman. She teaches English courses at the community college to help people qualify for admission. She likes the students and is well-liked at her job. Mostly I think she is happy, and certainly she is a good and charming person. I suppose she was drawn to my curly blond hair, blue eyes, and six-foot lightly nourished frame, which I still have. I know that I was attracted, and still am, by the perfection of her olive skin, light brown eyes, glossy brown hair, seductive mouth, and a way of moving that is somewhere between flowing water and clouds. Our bodies brought us together.

Our connections now have gone deep under the ground, unspoken and unquestioned. We no longer look into each other's eyes and move or speak or act out of that still place. Making love is rare and routine. We traverse our daily life together like goats on a path worn narrow into a hillside. We explore neither the heights nor the valleys, nor do we stray into the great plains of middle-range intimacy. Sometimes I forget she is here.

She does not know I consider killing myself. I don't think that keeping secrets is necessarily a bad thing or a mistake.

Our daughter, Sabrina, will graduate from Tulane next year. I don't see her often anymore, but when I do I swear she carries the fragrance of baby powder. Her youth and beauty stun me.

Sabrina, Dana. Obviously, killing myself is impossible. I could not hurt them so much. Nevertheless, I keep the possibility in my mind, as an emergency release valve. Also, I can write the notes.

A suicide note is for telling my life and what I am going through. Who are you, anyway? I can't see you at all. What if we wrote notes to each other? I could send you my suicide note, and you could send me yours. It feels stupid, me just flinging mine out in your direction with no return.

Tim

Being a shrink, naturally I've known people who have killed themselves. I also know people who try to kill themselves, and keep trying, and can't do it. It is bizarre.

Four months ago, I took a new patient for the first time in a long while. A year before I met him, he shot himself in the chest with a twelve-gauge shotgun. Two years before, he jumped off a high bridge. He walks with a limp and has some trouble breathing, but against all odds, he's here.

Alan is sixty years old. His face is ruddy, and he wears his graying blond hair in a high-and-tight military cut with a curl at the front. His hands are pale, childlike, and he is too small for his baggy clothes except that his skinny legs are too long for his jeans. I'm guessing they shrank in the dryer.

At our first meeting, I introduced myself to him in the waiting room. He said nothing and never looked at me during the whole session. The second session was the same. Most of the time I joined his silence, sitting for an hour in what felt to me like a comfortable pause in the day. I would make small comments and occasionally ask a question, never acknowledged. But the third meeting was a leap forward in our relationship when he nodded at me in the waiting room and said, "Hi." At the fourth visit I smelled an unmistakable chewing gum flavor as he came in the door, and I commented: "Umm. Juicy Fruit." I saw the trace of a smile. He looked at me a few times during that session, and once, out of the blue, he made a mock scary face at me. I made a face back, arching my eyebrows in exaggerated surprise. He looked down. "Anytime you want to talk about anything, feel free," I said. He nodded.

Because of his suicide attempts, the system pays me to see him three times a week. Officially, since I have to give him a label for Medicaid, he is bipolar with psychotic features, and he also has post-traumatic stress disorder and social anxiety. During the first few weeks, he was usually silent and sometimes seemed so removed as to be catatonic. Once he seemed agitated, to the point of speaking in a confused psychotic language called "word salad." But his meds and my patience are helping, and now I'm getting to know a sweet, smart, funny guy who hates himself.

One day, he just started to talk. He was completely

coherent and appropriate and went right to the point about his suicide attempts. "I tried to kill myself. I found out it doesn't solve depression. I can't even kill myself. Every time I fail, my self-esteem plummets. And I feel more hopeless than ever. I can't even hope for death. It doesn't work." His legs shook back and forth with the side effects of his anti-psychotic pills. As always, I wondered what was the lesser evil.

A question came to me out of nowhere, and that is a place I trust. "What's the best thing that ever happened to you?"

He never answered a question before and he tensed up for a moment, but quickly his face softened, and he seemed to visit that nowhere place himself. "Once I was in a grocery store. It was a few years ago. I was walking down the aisle, and there were these cans and bottles, and other people were in the aisle too. And all of a sudden, I felt normal. I just felt fine to be there. Nobody wanted to hurt me or laugh at me or take my money. I just belonged there like all the rest of them."

I nodded. "You belonged there."

"Yeah."

"Such a good, ordinary way to be."

"Yeah."

Dear Friend,

I am thinking right now of my daughter, my only child, when she was a little girl, with her little tanned arms and legs animated in all directions like a cartoon puppy: the force that through the green fuse drives the flower. When I picked her up in play, her whole torso wiggled, and those little limbs would push against mine as if they could move the world. They surely moved mine.

I felt the same force in her more than a few times when I held her tight while she had a tantrum. Holding her not in frustration, not to stop her, but only to keep her safe from herself and let her know I was right there. Tennyson has a phrase, "nearer than hands and feet." He's talking about God, but I felt that way as her dad.

Now, I can't take care of anything. We have two cats who take excellent care of themselves. My wife holds and cuddles them, and we both put food in their dishes. Plants, which I would have thought would be easier than animals, turn out to be insidiously demanding. I don't know what they want and think that because they are so

21

still, they don't want anything. But over slow plant time, they turn brown or rusty or otherwise gloomy.

But I have discovered something I am able to take care of: rocks. I can't hurt them, or even if I do carelessly drop and chip one, it doesn't feel it. The sharp new corners and shiny exposed spot that used to be safe inside is suddenly now an outside face. This is startling for a while, but you know it is just all in the character of a rock to occasionally shift and fall and break a piece off and go on living just fine. They have so much time. They are bound to encounter some changes. They don't care. They seem happy, and they make me happy. I bring rocks home from anyplace I go where they are. I pick up small ones to carry for just a while and discard. They don't feel discarded.

Rock, paper, scissors. As much as I love rocks, give me paper every time. Scissors *cuts* paper, for god's sake. How violent is that? And rock *smashes* scissors: get the hell out of here, scissors. Smash you.

Paper just quietly, politely, covers. A temporary, gentle domination, the comfort of writing. Or a permanent solution, the suicide note.

Always,
Tim

"Depression is a fat man," Alan told me one day. He wriggled his very narrow frame in the chair. "He's a sumo wrestler. Sits on me. He's the heavyweight champ of the world."

"You can't get out from under him."

"Not today." He looked out the window for a while. I waited, feeling very heavy. Finally, he went on. "Sumo has two arms. One is uncertainty." He lifted his right arm, and his voice turned mocking. "It says, '*Maybe not, probably not. But then again, it could be.*' Nothing, absolutely nothing, is ever certain. Or even real. The other arm," he said, raising his left one, "is negativity." His voice became harsh. "'*It's no good, nothing's no good. You're no good. Actually you're shit.*'" He sat slumped over and frozen. "Everything hurts."

I knew what he meant. It hurts to move, to have five senses. Hearing things hurts, seeing things hurts. The air around you especially hurts. You hold very still. "It hurts," I said, "just being alive."

"Yes." He came up out of his crouch and glanced at me. "Sometimes I think you know too much about all this stuff. Sometimes I wonder if you've been here."

"Yeah," I said. "I can go to bad places." Every patient doesn't need to know this, but something in me understands that Alan can get inside me a little without it harming either of us.

He nodded and sank back into the chair, his chest caving in and arms dropped limp at his sides. It was a slow fade, like letting go of a raft and sinking below the surface of a lake. Bye-bye.

We sat for a long time without speaking. Finally, I asked, "How you doing over there?"

"Okay, I guess."

He wasn't. He wants to die. He wants to kill himself. He thinks he deserves it. And better he should hurt himself than suffer someone else hurting him. And he has a few other good reasons, the main one being that dying would be a relief, maybe. Maybe.

I wanted to start humming to him. I wanted to sing him a quiet song. Earlier that morning I had listened to some strange music from Estonia, laments and then celebrations, all in a mysterious language and the meandering solo voice of a woman. She was accompanied by a Jew's harp, drums, and a spectacularly crystalline stringed instrument that tinkled like melodic icicles.

Instead of humming, I stretched in my chair and asked, "What's going on inside you?"

It took a while, but we finally got to talking about him wanting to kill himself. I know he has a plan to do it, and he's not telling me this. He doesn't know that I wouldn't take away his plan. As long as it's just an idea and he's not acting on it, a plan could be a source of rest for him. I know what a relief it is to have one.

I thought he was too depressed to do it right then. The times he tried were done when he was manic and had the energy. When he left, I didn't think he would do it that day, and we arranged to check in the next day on the phone.

Dear You,

Last night I dreamed that Alan was going to be executed. It wasn't fair but it was out of my control. He waited for the time to come. I sat nearby. I was confused. I thought of going to sit with him but did not. I had no energy and wasn't sure what to do.

Then he was gone. It was done. I couldn't believe it,

but it was true: life, gone. I deeply regretted that I did not sit next to him. How could I have failed to do so? It would have meant something. I did not.

Can I find the way to sit next to myself?

Tim

Yesterday Alan was telling me about sitting along the river. "Leaves were falling on me."

The clock ticked, and wind moved the branches outside my window. I could see and feel his leaves, the river. "Leaves falling over you."

"Yeah. They were yellow." Silence for a while, then, "I kept the ones that landed on me." Sheepishly, "I thought words might be written on them, but there weren't any. Then I thought if I laid them down in order, the words might turn up."

"How did that go?"

"No words." He reached into his backpack and pulled out a thick book with a faded red cloth cover. "So I put them with some words to help them out." He laughed and gently fanned the pages to show me the aspen leaves pressed there.

"Lots of leaves," I said.

"Yeah, leaves inside leaves." He closed the book and started to put it away, then opened it again and turned the pages carefully, studying his collection. Some were brown, most were yellow, some were green with orange, a few were brilliant orange. "Still no words on them," he said. He picked out a large leaf, rich yellow with tinges of deep orange and green veins. "For you, Tim." He handed it to me. "Give it some words."

I twirled the stem between thumb and forefinger and watched the leaf turn. It was nearly weightless. Maybe a leaf is just a leaf, but this was a gift. At least for this moment, Alan trusted me. His trust felt like the light, lovely touch of the leaf itself. "Thank you. I don't know if I can give it words, though. They might have to come from you. But I'll see." Pause. "What's the book?"

He held it up: *The Collected Works of Edgar Allen Poe*. "It was the biggest book on the shelf at the house." Alan lives in a group home.

The leaf sits before me this morning, still wordless.

Dear Reader,

I'm eating a peanut butter and jelly sandwich at three-thirty in the morning. I woke up hearing noises in the house. The cats were both asleep on the bed with my wife and me, all hands accounted for. The noises were downstairs, intermittent, unidentifiable, not very loud. Lazily, I thought someone might be breaking in. More realistically, I guessed it was a ghostly visitation. I am haunted at times. Barely seen shapes flit past the edges of my vision; hissing voices come from nowhere. It scares the hell out of me, and I usually take a sleeping pill. But tonight, not because of the noises but because I was hungry and awake—and I confess, curious—I got up and came down here. Turns out there's nothing.

Are all psychiatrists as mad as this? No, I'm sure not. Having to deal with some of the same things patients have to deal with has both pros and cons. I'm not psychotic; my visitations are flashbacks, post-traumatic stress from childhood abuse.

But I wonder if there is also something else.

Wait, this is important. I've always lived at the edge of a very thin veil between worlds. Peanut butter and jelly helps me tonight to stay on this side. But if I don't explore the other side, I'm ignoring too much of myself. I'm depressing too much life.

Do you understand? I'm so drawn to the murk, the unconscious. What is that alluring place on the other side, all that life on the other side of the veil? What's over there that sends so frequent emissaries to me?—bits of hallucination, fleeting and frightening but energetic and bright in their darkness. Some are flashbacks, straightforwardly so: hotel room walls, Uncle Joe's white hairless shins. But these nasties mingle shamelessly with intimations of wisdom: the words on Alan's leaves.

I need to visit the kingdom by the sea. I ignore it at my peril. My work with patients takes me there, especially with Alan, who spends a lot of time in that place. I need to work the same way with myself. I want to find the words on my own leaves. The problem is that Uncle Joe guards the entry. His lewd smile dares me to enter my unconscious; his narrow, wet fingers grab at me. I cringe. I back off. I am depressed.

But I believe that going through to the other side is necessary. My life depends on it. This I believe, and I pray for the chance to go further.

Very sincerely,
Tim

Dear You,

I've taken to bed. All hours of the day and night, lying in wait for enlightenment from the darkness. A few times lately, I've taken that photo out of the bedside table drawer, looked at it for a while, then replaced it, without enlightenment but with some kind of conviction. *This*, I say to myself. *This*.

Yesterday afternoon Dana came in and sat on the side of the bed. "Tim, are you okay? You worry me."

"I do? Why?" I was genuinely surprised. I thought no one could see inside me from outside me.

"You're pulled back, more than usual even," she said. "But you almost seem happier. You're not as morose and lackluster as you've always been." She laughed, but then she got serious and asked again, "Are you okay?"

"I'm fine." I held up my thumb, which had a Band-Aid on the tip. "You fixed me, remember?" The night before, I had cut myself on a can lid. The bleeding wouldn't stop. I held a Kleenex over it, then another. I was going to bandage it, but Dana insisted on putting peroxide on first, which I can't stand to do because it stings. We held pressure some more after that, and she put the Band-Aid on. It bled through a bit but finally stopped.

"Really, I'm okay," I said, and right then, I was.

I got up and showered and dressed. But I can't make myself go out. It's been a year since I've played pick-up basketball at the park. Friends sometimes call and I talk to them like everything is normal but turn down dates for coffee. I need to go to work. I keep up with the few patients I have, but since taking on Alan, I've been turning down new ones. I've got to start returning calls. I need money. I need to go out.

Also, when I work, I get better. Without shame, I say that my work is good for me: *me*. I think it is also good for the people I see. Twice in the past week, a former patient has contacted me about sending records someplace, and each of them sounded glad to hear my voice and told me: "You helped me a lot." I know my work is good for all of us.

But I still wonder how badly I have failed patients— or worse, done damage. One of my patients told me one day that her G.P. had said she sounded depressed and he prescribed Prozac, which immediately helped her. I had never prescribed anything for her, nor done a formal assessment for depression, nor even used that word with her. Why? Because I took her troubled mind and loss of interest in life to be normal. *Normal.*

If I kill myself, that will count as a big failure as a therapist.

How wounded can a healer be and still be a healer? This question stirs a feeling in me. I believe in something here. Placebo—what I believe in—will heal me. What is it?

In college, I was in a bar by myself one Sunday afternoon watching the NBA playoffs. I was drunk and glued to the game on television and did not want to be bothered. A man in a business suit was drinking by himself a few stools down. He pretended to be interested in the game, but he wouldn't stop talking to me.

To be polite, I looked at him during a time-out and saw a face some decades older than mine, soupy eyes sunken into darkened flesh and a face shiny from close shaving. *Shit*, I thought. *Another old fucker wants me.* The game started again, but he kept talking. And then, one minute he was talking about his business deals, and the very next minute, he said, "My son killed himself last year," and left it at that.

The Bullets and Supersonics seemed far away. I looked at him. "I'm sorry."

"It's been hard, but my wife and I are moving on."

"How old was he?"

He cried and said twenty—my age—and took out a handkerchief and blew his nose. We went back to watching the game, and after a few minutes he paid and left. As he passed me, we nodded to each other, and I wasn't sure which of us had the son who died.

That old fucker pushed me over into medical school and psychiatry. I saw in the murk of his eyes what I believe in: that I am tied into a long thread that strings together, or knots together, all those who suffer and seek solace.

I'm often on fire with love for my patients. Sometimes I'm frozen with fear—for them, with them, of them. We are all in deep shit with no way out that I know.

We want to get out. We try to get out. Every forty seconds, someone on the planet commits suicide.

Sincerely,
The Believer

Dear Friend,

My daughter called last evening. She's twenty now, living in New Orleans, about to start her last year of college. I sat out back and talked to her under the willow trees in the yard, which is rocky ground that quickly blends out onto the slope of the foothills with their scrubby brush and stands of tall sugar pine. The horizon was a gentle pink with the sunset.

"I'm dying of the heat and I miss home," Sabrina said.

"Gone three years and still homesick? That's nice," I said. "That you miss us, I mean."

"I do. What's up with you, Poppa?"

"So little to do, so much time," I said. "Today I've been hanging around here listening to music."

"Oh, what is it?" She'll graduate next spring with honors in music. When she was four she loved listening to classical music. One day she begged to have a violin, and both she and her mother were shocked at my vigorous "No!" They didn't understand that I would not allow it because Uncle Joe had played violin. Sabrina was mad at me, but a few days later she heard Yo-Yo Ma. "*That* is what I want to play," she declared, standing in front of me and stamping her foot and scowling. She was surprised when I cheered "Bravo, baby girl!" Now, she is happiest when she is playing her cello on the streets. She dips and sways and hums. People can't resist stopping to watch and listen, and they leave with smiles on their faces.

I told her about the Estonian folk singer, then asked about her. I listened to her news and enjoyed the sound of her voice for a few minutes before my wife got home and came out to the yard. "Baby, here's your mom," I said. I handed the phone to Dana. I walked a little distance off and poked at a loose fence post. Dana started laughing and I sat down in the dirt, smiling.

After the call, we walked around the yard and felt the evening melting into night. We sat on a bench. The longer we sat, the more the land around us came to life: rustlings, and then all over the place, the more you looked the more they were there, the dull tiny glowing of some little worms that I never see, or think to look for, in the daytime. I only know they're worms because Dana said so. She picked one up in the dark one night when we first moved here.

"I want you to be happy," she said. "You kind of are, I think. But then I don't know."

I don't know what I said. In between quiet words about nothing, feeling her next to me, I knew I might touch her. But what was, was enough. "I'm happy to be with you."

Does this have a place in my suicide note? It's why I'm not writing one. The bench in the dark with Dana is my foot on the ground of caring. It was that way when Sabrina called. I have so little to say to her, but just getting to hear her voice is another foot on the ground of caring, about living.

Poppa

~~~

Dear Friend,

I'm up in the night again, peanut butter and jelly. Tonight I went to sleep with a very new sense. The words for it are, *I want the best*. This was the most amazing possibility. I liked it very much, having that kind of good wanting.

But now energy is dissipated, and I'm tired. I want sleep. That's what everybody who kills himself must want—good sleep.

Thick sludge without thickness. I can't get through it.

Try. Keep putting words on page. Writing is wanting to live more than wanting to die. Force that through the green fuse drives.

I want the best.

More awake now, waking up.

Earlier tonight I had a dream in which my uncle was drowning, and I jumped in to save him. Quickly it became me who was drowning, and I woke with a terrific fear as I was going down.

Dream: drowning, I didn't want to. Wild, animal fear. Primal NO against death.

Not yet ready.

Do I want to get ready?

Immediately, I challenge myself: what about if I get ready to live instead?

I might even write a great un-suicide note.

Tim

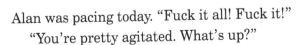

Alan was pacing today. "Fuck it all! Fuck it!"

"You're pretty agitated. What's up?"

"Nothing!" He stomped around the room. His energy was refreshing. "It's just anxiety. I'm anxious. Depressed too. They're the king and queen."

"King and queen of Alan-land today."

"Fuckers!" He stopped, leaned on a windowsill, and then finally sat down. "Fucking king and queen. When they fuck, it turns out they're sterile. Or they make a big globby baby called Chaos." The pacing had helped him. He lay back in the chair looking almost relaxed.

Anxiety is a contraction against an expansion that wants to happen. I asked myself what he wanted to expand into: anger at the king and queen, mom and dad, of course. I could have said, give 'em hell, Al, and had him bang a pillow. But instead, I asked him, "What do you want?"

"Freedom," he blurted. It startled him, and he straightened up.

"Say that again."

Long, long moments while he faced his terror of saying what he wanted.

I coaxed: "You can say it if you want to."

It came out as a whimper, but he managed it: "I want to be free. I want freedom."

Beloved Reader,

I hate to turn the light on, but it is hard to write a suicide note in the dark. I just got it dark and quiet. I unplugged the television, which had a blinking bright green light. The wall clock was loud. I closed the door to muffle it but could still hear it. I took it down and put it under a pillow on a chair.

So it was dark and quiet. Only the flickering bright grinning faces in my mind, only the never-screamed screams that live there. But if I'm going to write, I have to have a light on. So I gave up the dark, and here I am.

Tonight, I'm not feeling that bad. The faces, the screams, are more memories than living entities, as if they're also stashed under a pillow. I could even forget them. So I will.

What is here tonight is desire. Not that I *feel* it, though if I listened carefully at the edge of the pillow of my depression, I might. It's more words and images than actual feelings.

Well, I'll tell the truth. I have a visitor: a lovely man has come through the veil into my dreams. It is Peter

O'Toole, leggy, mouthy Peter. The Brit accent is so lovely, and he's aging nicely. Roguish, competent, fun-loving. Able and willing.

Erotic. In my dream, he and I were moving toward making love. I was more or less throwing myself at him, with no shame or blame anywhere. I take it to mean that I am *available* to "Peter of the Tool." My erotic power, to live and love.

Does this sound like a person damping down the ticking of a clock to have the necessary silence to write the perfect suicide note?

Peter wants me to come out and play. I know it is a hopeful sign, and I know that ignoring a clear and hopeful dream summons is a grave error. This is one place we have free will. Something is going on; something is available to me, and me to it. Peter wants me to use my energy, not depress it. *Use it.* Tool that I have.

But how can I fulfill this in the context of who I am? My habits of hesitation and holding back. My credit card debt, my absent social life. I *believe* I can do something, but there is a dismal side of me that doubts I will really take this thing very far. I might muster a cheese sandwich with avocado and pesto, instead of only lettuce and mayo. Or a trip to the mountains, or a half-baked effort to clean the house.

Sincerely,
Me

~⊃

Today, Alan lugged a guitar up my stairs. He left it in the case and talked about other things—complaints about a neighbor and mostly complaints about himself. He won't get out of the house. He won't stand up to his housemate who borrows his money and never pays it back. He won't stop thinking bad thoughts.

"Just won't," I said.

"Right." He sat without speaking for a while. "I won't play my guitar either." He looked at it. "But next time, maybe I will. I'll leave it here. Okay?"

First the leaf, now his music. "Fine. I'll keep it safe. Nobody will bother it."

"That's what I want."

"I know." Safety: the first human need.

~⌒～

Dear, dear, dear. Dear god someone,

Don't leave me here.

I am building a fire, and I am not able to remember my daughter's name. At first it seems unbelievable: of course I know it. I *must*. It is....

I can taste the name. I feel it in my shoulders and arms. Seeing the fire start up and then falter, shifting sticks with the poker. Another part of me—now it is my back and shoulders—is seeking the name. I know I know it.

The name, the name. I silently say her last name, my last name. Waiting to know what name comes before that: she is _____ Jones. _____ Jones.

Is it Sabrina? How strange. I think it is Sabrina; this is the dawning name, but it is totally unfamiliar. Sabrina, Sabrina. I say it a few times, and it dubiously locks into place but still doesn't seem right, although I know, distantly, that it is.

I'm swimming upstream, wanting to get back to Peter O'Toole. I want to lay my eggs in his wide smile and die.

But the current against me is so swift.

A few days ago, I finally took on a new patient. When he arrived, I thought I knew him from somewhere, but I couldn't place him. His speech was fast, meticulous. His eyes were those of a serpent. He was as cold as a man drowned in freezing water, rigid and fit, muscles bulging under a sweater. His stiff, shiny black boots were combat-ready. He was calculating, deadly, and as crazy as a loon. He scared me nearly to death. My chest shrank into a steel cube, and I could barely breathe.

His name is Wallace. He said he had been tortured as a POW in Vietnam and told me more details than I would ever want to know. He talked mechanically but with an intensity, and in among his long monologues of hatred for ex-wives, people in power, and queers and peaceniks, he occasionally slipped in references to me. Of how I was "probably one of that crowd" that he hates or how he might move his arms were he, for example, to strangle me.

I managed to speak and act with some decorum, though with no therapeutic value to him. When he left at the end of the session, I collapsed over my desktop. But moments later I leapt up, ran downstairs and outside. I saw him and he didn't, apparently, see me. He was

43

climbing stiffly into a dark brown van. It was shiny and completely opaque. I tried but couldn't read the license number, in an illusion of control, as if I might do something about him.

I've been sick since then. Lying in bed, I explored the steel girder that built itself in my chest. It went up so fast and with such strong purpose that it endured fully intact for a day. It would probably be there now if I hadn't been the best possible therapist with myself. I remembered that shield: it was my old protection, a way to hold my body so no feelings went in or out. I held it softly, willing to feel it, and allowed it to be there completely as long as it liked. My patience melted it away. When I got up, it was gone.

But the whole thing damaged me. I sit frozen by the faltering fire and try to comfort myself with the name I have remembered: Sabrina, Sabrina. I'm damaged, and Peter O'Toole is nowhere in sight. He's off starring in a new release of *The Pit and the Pendulum*.

So Lost,
Tim

Dear Friend,

Dana came home and found me asleep, moaning, curled up by the cold woodstove. "Do not tell me you are okay," she said. "What is going on?"

"Just that old stuff."

"Oh, that's all." She sat next to me, and we stared at the floor together.

"There's nothing to do about it," I told her.

She put her hand on my knee. "You seem to believe that. I'm sorry, but I don't believe it."

Placebo works in strange ways; maybe what *she* believes in can cure me. I asked, "What do you believe?"

Dana said nothing, but she stood up and reached her hand down for me to stand also. I did. She led me to the couch, pushed me to sit there, and kicked off her shoes. Then she knelt on the couch, straddling me. Her heart to my heart, her arms around my neck, her face turned and her cheek against my shoulder.

Tim, Finding My Way

Dear Who,

Wallace said he was tortured in Vietnam. Alan is a vet, too, but he was tortured long before that by his father. Alan learned how to get beaten daily. He learned that every word out of his mouth was the wrong one and that he must lose any argument started by his father. He hid in holes he dug in the sand of the dunes near their house.

Wallace drives that opaque brown van. Alan rides a red bicycle. Wallace is much crazier than Alan. His airtight paranoia far outdoes Alan's depression. They both have post-traumatic stress disorder. Alan suffers so much. Wallace can't find his suffering, but he knows it is there somewhere. He uses tremendous strength to lock it out, which is impossible, so it intensifies inside and torments him.

Both of them, really, are on the Wheel of Torture.

I found a better home for Wallace. I phoned colleagues and arranged to refer him to a therapist who is six foot four and rides a motorcycle. It's better for Wallace but the good part is, it's better for me. I don't have to put myself through things like that anymore. Somewhere, Peter O'Toole is smiling.

Me

～◦

I could not work with Wallace, but I enjoy working with Alan. I feel so much safer, happy even, with someone whose madness is acknowledged.

He played the guitar today. "This is my job. It's a fifty-minute-a-day, three-days-a-week job."

He used to do it for a living, and he's good. He diddled with a nursery rhyme tune for a while, gradually slid into the blues, then crashed the strings in a funny, elaborate flamenco. From there he played what seemed to be his own music, which ran the gamut in tone, pace, melody, or not. Watching him play, his ease, his discovery, did my heart good. The music itself was wonderful. That he played it with me—for me?—was another gift of trust.

He talked a little, still playing. "That guy in the house never paid me back that twenty-five dollars."

"He keeps doing that," I said. "Any ideas how you can keep your money for yourself?" Sometimes I try to help him learn to use good judgment, but he's really not interested.

Music for a while, and then he said, "I could bust him in the mouth."

I sighed and hung my head in comic despair. Alan laughed, and the music went on.

⸺ ♫

Dear You,

I lay in bed this morning and listened to the Estonian wailer, the songs of people who live in dark places. I wondered: if I could have played that music for my uncle, wouldn't he have stopped and listened? Couldn't I, surely, have stopped him?

I thought about that. He had to go to the dark places. The glazing over of his eyes, him turning into a different person and showing himself to me that way, that was his way of going through the veil. He had to go because it was there, and he wanted to see through it. Like I do.

I did finally stop him. I was fourteen when he sidled up to me at a picnic and said he planned to take me to Yellowstone that summer. I said, "No, thanks," words coming out of the nowhere place and startling me as much as him. He missed just a beat before grinning. "Oh, okay. Maybe you're too big for that," he said, and that was the end of the sexual abuse. But he never stopped treating me like he owned me.

And I never stopped wondering why I didn't say no during all those years before. Did I want it all along?

I turned the music off and lay listening to the quiet: a hum from somewhere in the house, the cathedral silence of the bedroom. Light sprinkled sporadically around the ceiling with the moving of branches outside the windows. Then, I had a quick memory I had long forgotten. I was seven or eight. It was Christmas at my house. Aunts and uncles, cousins, my brother and sister were everywhere, busy and noisy. My mother was very drunk and fretting darkly in the kitchen over potatoes. The golden turkey sat on a silver platter on the dining table. I stood in a doorway, my stomach hurting and my mouth watering. Uncle Joe in his three-piece suit was sharpening the glistening silver knife. When he stepped up to the table to carve, he told me to come stand next to him, and I had a strong vision of taking the knife and stabbing him. I ran upstairs to the bathroom and vomited.

After dinner he played his violin. Stiff as a board, sitting on the edge of the bench always provided for his concerts, he tuned endlessly as we all waited. When it finally came, the music was some obscure Schubert or Elgar unknown to the rest of us. Even while playing he hardly moved except for a mechanical tapping of his right foot.

Then he made me go out with him. "Let's take a drive and see the Christmas lights, Timmy." He parked on a hill with the sparkling spread of colors below and tortured me for an hour or so.

Today I lay in bed remembering that, and I cried: simple quiet tears without struggle. I knew the truth of my loneliness. I was not resigned, agonized, or deflated. I was not hopeless because I had no need to change it. I understood that humiliation, longing, and hatred are part of what it is to be human.

Also, I knew that as a child I could not have stopped him. I pulled the photo out of the drawer and stood up, turned the music on again, and stood at the window shivering in my sweats, T-shirt, bare feet on floorboards. Outside, white cumulus lay over the mountains in the clearest blue air. The room behind me was filled with percussive and tinkling instruments and the fluid, yearning female voice singing crisp words of no meaning to me.

With Peter O'Toole at my side, I raised my arms up in

a wide embrace of it all and spoke out loud: "This is for you, Uncle Joe." Reverently, I tore up the photograph.

Tim

⁌⁍

"Tim!" Alan was jabbering before he was halfway up the stairs. "I went out yesterday!" A large plastic bag rustled against his knees with every jerky step. He dropped it onto the floor beside him as he plopped into the chair. "I went for coffee at Starbucks!"

"That's great!" This was truly big news for a guy who leaves his room only to pick up his Social Security check once a month, buy food and cigarettes, and come here three times a week.

He went on. "Yeah, I got a coffee and sat outside at a table. These two old guys at the next table, my-age-old, ha, were talking about some guy who was the son of an astronaut, and when he was a kid he hung around the space place in Houston, and now he's a multimillionaire. He made multimillions making video games. And so now he's just paid some people about half of his money to go up into space for two weeks. He said, now I'm like my father.

"Then this couple sits down. She's talking about her friend who can't decide which dress to buy. The friend is going to be the mother of the bride. The man says it's ridiculous that people spend a hundred thousand dollars on one day. The woman says but you did it once. He says he didn't know about that because he didn't pay for it. Then he said, 'Her parents would have paid a lot to get rid of her.'"

Alan's laugh was not his usual sardonic chuckle or occasional belly laugh. This laugh today was high and strained. I tried to get his attention—"Alan? Hey…"—but he talked over me.

"Wait, I need to tell you this part. I'm having a good time hearing these conversations, and then a guy comes up with a puppy on a leash. We're sitting outside. The lady whose friend is the bride's mother says how cute the puppy is. The man says yeah, they're cute when they're little but when they're big they're a lot to handle. Too much, he says. And all of a sudden, I realize he's talking about my penis."

That took me by surprise. Alan was looking right at me. "Wow," I said. I looked back at him. There was no recognition or contact in his eyes, and he quickly looked away, out the window.

"Yeah. And I get real scared. I'm about to have a panic attack because he's talking about me like that. But then I think, *the son of a bitch! What right does he have to talk about me like that*?" His eyes were open wide. "Right? Who's he to be talking about me? Right? What a jerk."

"Alan? Hey." I leaned toward him, but he wouldn't look at me. "You're going through a lot today." My talking was slow and quiet.

I saw his breathing start to calm, and he was quiet for a moment. "So much happened at that coffee shop! And I only had one cup." His laugh was softer.

I smiled at his touch of humor, still talking slowly: "Seems like it was a strong cup." His knees were pumping rapidly up and down, his fingers twitching, and his feet jiggling. I nodded toward his feet. "Want to run away? Or kick somebody?"

Another soft laugh and a pause. The feet came to rest. "There was so much those people said in ten minutes. There was enough to write songs about for a week."

I sat back and crossed my legs. I gestured at his guitar, leaning against the wall where I place it before his sessions. "You could do that." Silence. "Hey. Play a little guitar."

He picked it up and twanged a few hard, discordant sounds but quickly settled into smooth melodic routines. He started making up a song: *"The bride she had no pride. She let her parents sell her. I tried and I tried, I wanted so to tell her that her dad goes out in space 'cause he's trying to win a race, he won't look her in the face. All he wants is to find a place. All she wants is to find a place. All I want is to find a place, have a place, have a place."* He stopped and his hands fell limp on his lap. "I just wanted to go out and have a coffee, but it was too much."

That made me sad, and I had no response. Finally, I asked him what was in the plastic bag he had brought in with him. Manics are agitated, often angry, and they go on sprees of all sorts. He showed me his Salvation Army purchases: five cloth napkins, a giant bath towel, two scrub brushes. It seemed like he wanted to clean things up. There was more: two umbrellas, a bag of assorted used shoelaces, and a red sweater. "I've never seen you wear red," I said.

He stuffed it all back into the bag. "When I jumped off the bridge, I was on a run way worse than this." Good—he sees how his process of disintegration works, recognizes the lead-up to suicide. He was perched on his toes, heels jiggling, but his torso was sunken back into the chair.

"Let's not have you get to that."

"Right."

He agreed we could adjust his meds, and I phoned in the prescription.

"Hey, what that guy was saying about me? Do you think he really was talking about me?" Also good, he's seeing how he might be distorting reality.

I shook my head. "Uh-uh. I don't think he was talking about you at all."

"That's what I wondered. You don't think so?"

"I wasn't there, but from what you've told me, I'd bet that he wasn't. Talking about you. But I know you thought he was. It seemed to you that he was."

"Okay." He jiggled his legs for a while and finally took a deep, natural breath.

"Listen," I said. "I'm going to call you tomorrow morning to see how you're doing. Will you call me if you get crazy? No matter what time it is. If you start going off any deep ends whatsoever. And certainly if you're going to hurt or kill yourself. Will you?"

"I will." He went down the stairs with his load and looked up at me from the bottom. "Thank you."

My phone rang at ten that night. His voice was a wail. "Tim, I'm fucked. Just fucked."

"You're at home?"

"Yeah. I'm sorry, I'm sorry. I just shouldn't be alive. I'm sorry."

"Have you done anything, taken anything?" Silence. "Alan? Tell me. Have you hurt yourself or tried to kill yourself?"

"No." He broke into wails and sobs. "I'm sorry, I'm sorry."

"Hey, Alan. I think I'll come over. Stay there, okay?"

"I'm sorry…."

"Alan. You kept your promise to call me. Now will you promise to wait right there until I get there?"

"Fuck. Yeah." He screamed and hung up.

Protocol would have me call 911 and let them take him to Emergency. But being out of your mind and then getting hospitalized on top of it is nothing to go through alone. I went to his house and we called 911 together and then I followed the police car to the hospital. I stayed with him as long as they'd let me.

Talking and making music in my office help him. Meds help. But none of that is enough. Sometimes it all goes haywire, and nothing can fix it. This time he made a different decision than he had ever made before. He called. I answered. The hospital will keep him from killing himself, and I think he is healing.

***

Dear You,

I had a dream last night, something like a dream, but maybe I was awake. I was lying in bed, and I thought of something I had never thought of before: maybe he did it with other children too. I wasn't the only one. Faces of strange boys and girls rose out of a swamp and fell back in as I fell asleep—or fell someplace—and there was Uncle Joe, leering at other children and touching their penises, vaginas. I crumbled inside. I was *jealous*. I wanted his attention only for me. He turned toward me, and I wanted him to take me away and take my clothes off and fuck me, forever. I *did* want it.

Lying there in bed, I was terrified. I couldn't breathe. I was on the verge of running away but told myself: *Walk through the veil, Tim. You can feel this. It won't kill you to feel it.* I opened up to it ever so slightly, and in a gush, something melted away. The pain was still there, but it became *exquisitely* intense. My uncle stood there grinning, and I stood there feeling my terror and my wanting. My sex. Knowing it was truly mine. Not his.

The next thing I know, Uncle Joe is gone and I'm with Peter O'Toole, flirting, starting to hug and touch. I feel our bodies together. The tease and the turn-on are exquisite, and it is ME.

Me

Dear my dear one,

Tonight, I'm up again but not bothered. I'm eating peanut butter and drinking herb tea, petting the cat, stepping outside to look at the stars. I don't want to kill myself. I'm only writing to say hello.

Twinkle twinkle little star how I wonder who you are. Hello, out there! Hello! I see you; do you see me? Can you read my letter?

I hear you answering me. My skin is vibrating. That's a rustle from the wind of your breath. Back inside the kitchen, there is nothing *but* your answer. The salt and pepper shakers on the windowsill: it's you. Stuff strewn across the tablecloth—a bit of wrapping from a gift Dana fixed up tonight for a friend of hers, a cloth napkin tossed aside, basket of bananas, small vase of flowers, cup holding tea, empty plate, jar of peanut butter. My hand, holding pen, writing to you. Looking at these things, I see nothing but you. Looking at these things is hearing your answer. No matter where I look, my skin tingles and it's you. This isn't mania because I'm so calm. I have no desire to go anywhere or get anything, and I'm not haunted at all.

Everything is ordinary. The other day I was eating lunch at a deli. Styrofoam plate, plastic fork. The food tasted absolutely great. I understood that nothing was required of me—*nothing was required of me*—and I was held and existed in perfect grace and love.

My letter is foolish. Still, I hold it up to the veil so you on the other side can see it. I'm grinning, holding my page up to the veil and so happy to tell you these things on the page. They aren't truly foolish, though to normal people in the daylight they might seem so. They are as un-foolish and excellent as bits of wrapping paper, baskets of bananas, jars of peanut butter. You can read my language, and I can feel your breath tingling my skin. We are happy together.

Love,
Tim

I'm back. I've been away for a while. I took some time off with Dana. We stayed home and fixed the house up and took hikes. Early winter is the best because there are no tourists and no snow bunnies. We gave our boots over to the gray mud, hosed them off at night, and had fires. We remembered how to make love. To my surprise—and hers, I'm sure—she's the center of my life now. She always has been, but now I see it. I looked at her in the kitchen this morning: a frumpy little woman wearing two different plaids, her sleep clothes, shoulders slumped and hair stringing down as she bent over to pour her coffee. She spilled some, said "Shit," and as she reached for a sponge, I encircled her in my arms and inhaled her unwashed hair.

One morning I got up very early and thought that doughnuts would be just the thing. I got dressed, and before leaving I went back to the bedroom and looked at Dana. She was lying half onto her stomach, so totally buried in the covers that only her eyelash and brow proved she was there, and the mess of shiny hair curling out from the edges of the pillow she was under.

"Would you like a doughnut?" I whispered. "No, probably not. I'll get you one anyway. What kind would you like?" She was oblivious. "Okay, I'll pick one for you at the shop. Bye." I touched the duvet over what might have been her foot.

It wasn't even sunrise. I was surprised at the traffic out so early as I drove all the way downtown and out the other side on a wide, crowded boulevard, enjoying the drive and heading for the only doughnut shop I knew of. I passed a liquor store and an empty lot with high yellow grass and spotted the corner shop, identified by a neon *DONUTS* sign in the window. Fluorescent lights were on inside. Parking was easy on the side street.

The overpowering fragrance of sugar and frying oil assailed me when I opened the door. There was one customer inside, a woman. The man behind the counter was bent over, reaching inside the glass case. Using tongs, he

61

pulled out a maple long john, wrapped it in tissue paper, and carefully placed it in a white bag. He reached in again with the tongs and extracted a jelly doughnut covered with powdered sugar, wrapped it, and put it in the bag. As he moved across the floor to another glass case, I saw his shoes: shiny black combat boots. Just what you need in a doughnut shop. Even before he stood upright, I remembered the bulky chest and arms that were way too muscular for doughnuts. When he straightened, I saw that the short-sleeved light blue shirt was monogrammed in script: *Wallace*.

He rang up the woman's purchase and as she left, he turned to me. "Hi. What can I get for you?" An interested face, friendly customer-service eyes, with no apparent murderous intent. Nor any trace of recognition.

"Hi," I said. I hadn't thought about what to buy and bent over to look inside the display case. "Let's see...." He waited patiently. "I'd like two cake doughnuts and two glazed, please."

He selected, wrapped, bagged, and rang me up. I paid; he gave me change. I left.

Walking to the car, I marveled at myself shaking inside: the long-enduring energy of trauma. I marveled also at how many of us completely crazy people go about the world functioning normally.

~⊙

Alan didn't show up for his first appointment after he was discharged from the hospital. After fifteen minutes I called the phone at his house, and he answered after the first ring. "Hello?"

"Alan, it's Tim. I thought we had an appointment at two."

"Oh, yeah."

I waited for more and then said, "Can you come now? Or should we schedule another time?"

I heard him swallow. "I was thinking maybe I don't need to come anymore."

"Oh." I'm startled, and mad. This happens; people just stop coming. Stopping therapy is a decision that impacts their lives and deserves a searching assessment, but they treat it like nothing. Not to mention, it is a relationship. Don't we even get a proper goodbye? "Would you come in and talk it over?"

"What do you think? Do I need to keep coming?"

"I think it's your call. I'd like to know more about where you're coming from. It seems too big to talk about on the phone. Maybe it makes sense to stop therapy right now, or maybe it doesn't. Maybe you want to come less often. If you do decide to stop, it would be good to have at least one more meeting. A little closure."

"I just don't know if I need to keep coming. They gave me new meds in the hospital."

"We could set up one more appointment, and you could think about stopping or coming less often. Three times a week is a lot."

"I think maybe I'll just stop."

What the hell's going on? He's all fixed? Or he's mad at me, probably for getting him into the hospital, which is a humiliating, oppressive experience. I wonder if he's lost any trust he had in me.

Or maybe he just needs to do his own thing. Yes, that for sure. "Okay, I get it. Sort of. I wish I understood it more, but you're pretty clear. You don't have to come. But listen: you could have an appointment if you want it, anytime. Just give me a call if you want."

Nearly palpable relief from him; he actually sighed, letting out his held breath. "Okay. Thanks, Tim. Thanks for everything."

"You're welcome. I've appreciated your work in therapy, and I've liked getting to know you." More work in therapy could help him go further, but I trust that he knows what is best for him. I'm mad, and I'll miss him. But I can let him go.

"Okay. Goodbye, Tim."

Alan called a few days after we talked. He decided to come once a week. Both of us will go through our darknesses again, but over time it will be less—less often, less troubling.

His number came up for subsidized housing, and he moved from the group home to his own apartment. But, as will happen, his tormenters follow him no matter where he goes. He no longer has to put up with the guy in his house who talked him out of his money, but last weekend someone moved in below him who plays the TV loud all night and snarls at him when he goes down the stairs.

He looks bloated these days, fattened up from medication and his mostly crummy diet. He keeps his guitar at his apartment but brings it every session and plays for a long time. Today it was complex, astounding melodic music. Gypsy Alan. It's his way of going through the veil.

During a pause, he looked at me and said, "I know I'm here!" and we both had a good laugh.

He's taken up fishing. He gives me credit for it, which pleases me though I only heard him mention how he used to like to fish with his dad, and I urged him to go do it. He never does anything I suggest, but he did this. He bought a license and now spends most of his extra money on rods and reels and bait and special packs to carry it all in. He takes the bus out early every morning no matter what the weather is, then goes home for a nap and lunch, and then goes back to the river every evening. He talks about the water and the reflection of the trees.

It makes him happy, and it's improved his diet immeasurably. If he catches more fish than he can eat, he gives them to other people fishing there. But yesterday he did something different. "I caught a big one right after the sun went down, and a woman down the bank wanted me to give it to her. I told her no."

I was startled. "That's not a word you use that often," I said.

Alan crossed his legs at the ankles and looked at the floor. "No." We both laughed. He looked up at me. "Yeah," he went on. "I tossed the fish back in. I told the lady, I'm gonna give him one more day."

BIRTHDAY PRESENT

Yesterday I saw into an eighty-year-old woman—
her name is Violet Corcoran—who was seeing
into me. I was peeling off my gloves after finish-
ing her exam, and she was looking at me. "I'm going to
go home," she said. "Up to Tennessee." She has emphy-
sema and had just calmly said "no" to the possibility of
surgery. She doesn't want any more to do with doctors
or medicines. Her face was soft and her eyes looked like
they knew me, and they invited me to acknowledge that
I knew her, too. I looked back at her in that same way,
and she knew she was heard and believed. When she left,
both of us were at peace.

Often I see into patients like that, and sometimes they
see me back. Such meetings are the reason I've been able
to keep working in this deadly world of medicine.

As I watch the sun rising over the ocean this morning,
I remember where I learned that kind of meeting. It was
exactly forty years ago, October the twenty-seventh. It
was my birthday, though I had told no one. Today is no
different in that way. I keep privacy, perhaps to a fault,
and I have kept the memory of that night away even from
myself. Every birthday since that one is a reminder of
that event, and I always hurry past it back into forget-

ting. Not only on birthdays but whenever I have thought about this thing, I have allowed only fragments to present themselves before I push them away with confusion about what happened and shame at how I betrayed myself. Sometimes I think it was rare and precious, and other times I believe it was nothing but a devastating attack. Maybe I'm also unwilling to face the trauma. But today I want to look at the whole event, deliberately. I want to devote myself to it. Why? Yesterday, Violet woke me. I'm getting older. I will lose it soon enough. I want to have it now. Settling into my chair by the window, the Atlantic stretching endlessly before me and a refreshed cup of tea next to me, I close my eyes and remember.

I was living in Boston, doing my residency in medicine. Around three o'clock on a Tuesday afternoon, I took the elevator from the ICU to the basement. As I pushed through the door at the back entrance into the cafeteria, I brushed against a man standing at the condiment bar. He was lithe and narrow but solid. His body registered my intrusion—did he turn toward me? The hood was up on his dark blue sweatshirt, and he smelled of soap and leaves. I whisked through the cafeteria with a tray and took my beef Stroganoff to a back table in the corner where I liked to sit because it was away from the noise of the vending machines and out of the main traffic paths.

Right then I especially wanted to be apart from everyone. One of my patients had died that morning. He was a seven-year-old boy—his name was Jimmy—whose internal injuries were too severe after the car he was riding in and the rest of his family were demolished by a drunk driver. Emergency had stabilized him, and he arrived in the ICU collapsed on a gurney and buried under a ventilator, accompanied by wheeled drips. Nurses added an infusion pump and surrounded him with monitors. When I got to him, I saw a small, captured space alien lying helpless and yearning for his other world. I gave my orders for meds and monitoring. Before moving on to the next patient, I pressed my hand on his arm. A few hours later, a beeping monitor sounded as his blood pressure suddenly collapsed. We sprang into the bustle of fruitless action compelled by the imperative to save a life. But before a new drip could be secured, he died. "We did all we could for him, poor little guy," said a nurse.

Boy dies. Six years into hospital work, I put him into a bulging back pocket of lost patients and I marched on, with mocking self-recrimination that I had turned my back on other careers. I could have been a sculptor or a dancer. Or a boxer: during my internship I had found the hospital gym where I depleted myself every day on a heavy bag, the only evidence of wisdom in the place.

In the cafeteria I sat down, paused to gather myself, and opened a journal to finish reading an article but found I could only pretend to read, unable to dispel from my fingers the feel of the boy's throat when I searched for a pulse no longer there.

The man I had bumped into carried his tray to a table where he had left a pack, a few empty tables away from mine. His sweatshirt hood was back and hair draped to chin length in black waves along the side of his face. His hair looked wet.

We nodded at each other. "Hi," I said, though I wanted to be alone. I quickly dropped my attention back to the journal.

"Hi." He sat down and bent forward to devour a pork chop.

My mind would not stay with the journal and moments later I was staring into space, more or less in his direction. It must have seemed that I was looking at him.

"What are you reading?" he asked.

Startled, I glanced at the title and reported it: "Diabetic Cardiomyopathy." I made a face. "It's not as good as it sounds."

He laughed and we looked at each other for longer than should have been comfortable. I saw quick subtle changes in his face, light and shadow dancing across bronze skin. His eyes wanted nothing, threatened nothing. They searched and invited.

When I looked at the hungry man sitting near me, I saw someone who was free of deceit. Of course, I didn't know anything about him. But he was from outside. He was unencumbered by our dutiful work to heal, which we did by contorting, ruining. At the hospital, our talk with each other was banter and platitudes, to cover up the agony we felt with the pain we were immersed in. The way this man looked at me reminded me there was another way to live.

I hate saying that. It isn't supposed to be so, because later that night he broke into my apartment and assaulted me. But this morning as I am letting the truth out of its old cage, I know that our looking, and later his attack, made me a doctor who understands that hurt does not need to close us from what is bigger than that.

I know also that later, the touch of his hands was a balm to me. There in the cafeteria, I noticed his hands. Hands show age; I think he was younger than me.

I open my eyes and watch my own hand now as I pick up my cup, and I see that my veins protrude and have a slight shine. Back then, the running of my blood was less labored, and my veins were pale blue tracings in my hands, legs, feet. My skin was smooth, and in the hours we spent together his caresses released the muscles held tightened underneath, bringing me to a wide expanse of peace.

I have had exquisite sex many times in my life. Being with him was not more special or better in that way, though something about the bluntness of his touch was memorable. To this day I can feel it, quick and direct. And just as I still feel the imprint of his touch, I've also never left the fear behind. This morning I woke with it clenched as usual in my jaw. I breathe and relax it. It comes back, and I relax it again. Often I ignore it. I was a doctor then, and I'm a doctor now. I take charge of situations easily. I enjoy my life. I read. I listen to music. I have dear friends. I have had kind boyfriends, fine lovers, two of them my partners for long periods of time and still now my friends. Living alone now is my choice.

Lying in my hammock this morning, I rest in the blessing of being a man who is growing old in this place. The endless mesa lies around me. The reds and grays of the grasses and earth are dotted with stands of pine. Lazy, I watch the mountains out to the east: purple giants in a seething cloud bank that is perforated by slats of white gold light from a low rising autumn sun. The mountains are always there. When I look up from tying my shoe or washing the car, they stand. Yes, I am a lucky man. My girlfriend says she doesn't believe in luck and that we make whatever comes to us. I smile and challenge her to guess when I might have made Arizona. "Believe me," I tell her, "I never made Arizona."

She has been my best friend now for some years, yet there are things I've done in my life that she will never hear about even though I live with their memory as consistently as I live with the mountains. Whenever I think of these things, my breath clutches and my vision blurs with almost-tears. It seems possible that I did those deeds just so I could later find out, by the astonishing fact of the inkling of remorse that has no end, that I am a true person who does have a heart. I can't yet easily face what I did in Vietnam. I've gotten used to the nightly awakenings and the daytime hauntings, so many years now, but I can't face any closer look at that time. And I also push away the memory of the woman in Boston. But as I rest in the hammock today, she presents herself to me. It's October, after all.

Out on the mesa, three deer are browsing. Many animals live out here with me—snakes and lizards, bear, coyote, deer. Every spring, a pair of foxes returns from lower ground to have their kits in the juniper. The four or five young chase one another up and down the scrubby trees. One of the parents is missing a foreleg, but he, or she, gets around very well.

Cats live here, too: bobcats and the rare puma. There are also some feral cats. Two of these have come around and become tame—a soft light gray cat with a faint shadow of stripes, and a fuzzy yellow one with a black spot on one front paw. They finish off the milk in my morning cereal bowl after I'm done with it. The yellow one stretches out on her back to sleep on the rug or on the dirt. The gray never does that. She will perch on the top of a rock or on a bookshelf, which the yellow never does. Yellow is fuzzier than gray.

Both these cats kill. Every day, tiny gray birds and several different kinds of mice and voles end up terrorized and then dead. How can such lovely creatures do such harm?

From the hammock my foot dangles near the ground, and one of the cats saunters over to rub against it. His push is slight but definite, and memory turns to the way I stroked her neck and shoulder with my thumb, barely touching her skin, which was as soft as skin ever was. But I also hurt her. When I forced myself into her apartment and later when I struck her in the face, I saw complete terror. I would not do again what I did then. I was a different person, crazed and compelled. But beneath the meanness of my attack on her, something else wants to be known. I close my eyes: yes, there it is, a slight stirring below my heart, barely perceived. I open my eyes and see the cat, moving unheard on his way. That shiver in my belly is like the footstep of the cat onto the silent dirt between two dry leaves.

Forty years ago in Boston, I trapped and terrified a woman. But that is not all that I did. And although I find no end to my shame, I want today to follow the path to the goodness. That sensation I find now in my belly, like the cat's footstep, is the way.

I lived a few blocks from the hospital. After my shift, after being restored by battering the bag at the gym, showering, and eating a Tiger's milk bar, I headed home in the early evening. I looked forward to having the next three days off. Laundry needed doing, and grocery shopping. I could clean the apartment and resume reading a good book.

I saw him again at the front entrance. I was glad when he began walking my way, and we went along together with bits of small talk. Red maple leaves covered the sidewalks, and through the bare trees you could see a red line of sunset across the sky. I loved the chill, so cold it hurt my nose.

He left me at the corner of my small street with a terse "bye" and hurried on, his leaving as abrupt as an unexpected death. I let myself into my building, walked fast to the end of the hall, and went into my apartment, the last one on the left on the ground floor. I threw my purse and coat on the couch and pushed my shoes off with my feet. I pulled the Venetian blinds shut and turned the knob on the radiator. It started hissing and banging, and as

I opened my kitchen cabinet for tea, there was a knock at my door.

No one answered when I asked who it was. I opened the door, and he was upon me. He kicked the door closed, covering my mouth with one hand and with the other grasping my hair. He was talking to me. "Don't be afraid," he said. "You don't have to be afraid." I was as furious as I was terrified at this fool who was doing this thing that could do nothing but create utter, abject terror and at the same time tell me I didn't need to be afraid. And not only was I afraid and furious, I remember now that I thought what he said was funny.

I got away and flung a lamp at him, tripped, grabbed at the wall, and screamed. I kicked like hell and kneed at his groin and got in one good punch before he grabbed me and held me close, covering my mouth again. We stumbled backward, somehow not falling, and he pushed me through the hall into the bedroom and down upon my bed. I bit his hand, but he kept it on my mouth, letting me bite it hard, viciously, and still talking to me. "It's okay, you're okay. Don't be afraid." Suddenly I wondered if I was crazy for attacking this person who was no longer hurting or assaulting me, only holding me. His voice was soft and believable, and his eyes were looking at me in the way they looked at me earlier that day: seeing me, wanting to be seen, and inviting me to go someplace I needed to go.

I was just back from the war. I killed a lot of people during my three years in Vietnam, numerous enemy boys who looked very much younger than I was, twenty-two when I left. They discharged me out of Fort Devens in Massachusetts, certified free of disease, three thousand miles away from my home. I started hitchhiking, going north and then south and then north again, west, then east. I prowled freeways and the edges of towns over months of uncharted time, keeping to myself. I was used to occasional heroin and marijuana and had no trouble finding it.

Like any combat vet, I was shaken by sudden loud noises, but it was the absence of shock that was truly unbearable. Deep silence was not a problem as long as it held the possibility of quick destruction like a patrol, a solitary mission. When days went by and nothing happened, I became troubled, and I myself would become the source of the necessary explosion. I fought with men at a construction site, threw bricks at passing cars. Half-heartedly determined to kill somebody, I once jumped off a bridge into a fast-moving river. With great effort I saved myself, though I lost a warm coat and a pair of boots.

I had learned early in my life how violence could be an instrument of many different things: meanness, bravery, protectiveness, good sense, confusion, anger, and love. Children were not seriously hurt where I grew up, but no one stopped us when the sudden sharp turns of anger that rose up in our bellies rushed out into kicks and striking fists. One time an uncle was smashing holes in the walls of his trailer, first with his fist and then with a wrench. My aunt became furious and stabbed him with a large knife. He staggered a little and then stood up stiffly and toppled like a tall tree falling straight over. I thought he might die, and he did.

I was eleven. I left and walked the long gravel road down to the county road, turned right toward the Pine Tree Store, and walked past it for some miles. Flower petals from plum and dogwood landed on snowmelt along the sides of the road. I walked the six miles to the river and watched the flood of it until dark and then, freezing cold, I went home. I felt strong and completely alone. I knew I would be all right, even though I had just seen my uncle die.

But that day in Boston, none of this helped me. I needed not more violence but a place to find ease. The night before I got into Boston, I was at a highway rest stop and a man was slapping his son. I threw the bastard off the boy, stepped hard on the man's face, kicked him a few times, and left. A creek was running through the rest stop. I made my way upstream through the brush for some distance, where I threw down my pack and vomited hard in the bushes and then went into the cold, shallow water. I waved off bugs and doused myself, rubbing mud over my skin and into my hair, half a year grown out from the military cut, then rinsing. I got out, dried off, and slept the night. In the morning I sat in the grass for hours. Sunlight waved in the creek's ripples, and ripples of moving light waved on the underside of bushes hanging over the water.

I hitched into Boston. Hospital cafeterias have cheap hot food. I found a hospital, went in, and bathed long and carefully using a men's room sink. I put on clean clothes. I went to the cafeteria and was standing at a counter pumping ketchup onto my fried potatoes when a woman barely grazed me as she came in through a door beside me. Already past me, striding toward the stack of trays, she waved out her hand, fingers splayed and for a moment holding their place in the air, a gesture of apology.

I watched her. There was no line, and she went along the display of food exchanging greetings with the server, naming her quick choices, arriving at the register and paying with bills folded up in a pocket of her white jacket. I admired the economy and purpose in her crisp movements. She was slight but stood tall. When she turned, I was surprised to see that her face, cradled by short, shiny blonde hair, was a troubled one, pale, with sunken eyes. She looked like a person in mourning.

Most of the tables were empty, but she walked to the far end of the room and settled near the table where I had left my pack. When I came back, she glanced at me and said hi before turning to her plate and a magazine. I was eating and noticed when she stopped reading and started looking at me. Needing to say something, I asked what she was reading. She made a joke, we laughed, and we looked at each other.

It was not a staring or a seduction. It was a looking into. We said a few words, but for a year or two after coming back from Vietnam, I could barely talk at all: yes, no, what's the way to the park, hi. I learned to smile sometimes, but I didn't smile at her. I did know that our looking mattered.

She left the cafeteria before I did. I dawdled, glad to be sitting down in a warm place, nowhere to go. After about an hour I left and walked the halls on every floor, sat in hallway chairs, picked up magazines but put them down quickly. The colors and headlines made me dizzy. Walking again, I stopped and looked at the pictures on the walls. That was all right.

I ended up in the lobby and sat there wondering where to go next. Just as I was walking out the front door, she appeared. We looked at each other again, same way, and walked out together and down the sidewalk.

"Beautiful night," she said.

"Yes." The sidewalk was hard. Cars were zipping past on the street, and on the parallel highway alongside. I knew I should say something. Invite her for dinner? Very funny. It would be impossible for me to go through an evening or a month trying to make nice with someone who most likely would not have given me the evening, much less the month. When she turned onto a side street, I walked onward as if I knew where I was going. A few steps farther, I turned back. I stashed my pack between a wall and a bush and followed her.

~ ⸙

I quickly found I was powerless to stop this thing. Once we had fallen onto the bed, I fought for only a minute and then stopped, realizing that I was being touched in a way that was not meant to hurt me. He was kneeling on the floor, half on top of me. With one hand he held my wrists on the pillow above my head, just tightly enough to keep them there. The other hand petted my hair back away from where it spilled onto my face.

"I only want to hold you," he said. He moved his thumb and fingers across my cheeks and lips, then traced my clavicle and tapped lightly over my heart: knocking to be let in. "I need you. Just to hold me. I won't hurt you."

"Why would I believe you?" Yet, I did. "You broke in. You *did* hurt me." Speaking to him began to quiet my pulse and breathing.

"I'm sorry." He was looking into me again. Then: "Let's be quiet."

I didn't want to talk either. I didn't want to reason

or convince, cajole or plead. I didn't want to get to know anything about him or tell him anything. I held very still. I was still afraid, frozen with the shock of his attack, but inside I was warming. The soles of my feet felt as if they were burning.

He let my hands go and took off his sweatshirt. I left my hands where they were.

He was beautiful. His shape was fine, his muscles evident. His skin was dark gold, and the hair on his body nearly invisible. His chest was seared with contracture scars from burns. On his throat were scars, many fine ones and one short streak of lumps from shrapnel wounds. His cheekbones were strong, the left one dented from an injury. His lips were full. His fine black hair was streaked with copper. His eyes were light brown and at one moment intense and inquiring, the next moment patient. Once he closed his eyes and his face then belonged only to him, to something inside him.

It may be that his beauty mesmerized me and is still doing so. But when he appears sometimes in my dreams, I don't even see the muscled body or the dark beauty of his features. It is another quality altogether that draws me: warmth like a bonfire in a dark countryside, steady, large, radiant. And something else: a quietness. It seemed to me that this man needed nothing. What a strange thing to say, of him who took so much.

But he is not here. I am sitting alone in a pleasant room lit by sunlight, with the ocean surging onto the stretch of beach outside. He is long and far gone. He will never be back, with his black silk hair that flowed across my milk skin. I think of a diamond, carbon so dense it bursts into brightest light.

What was I thinking? I wasn't. Following her came as easily as the cat now finds his journey around the low wall where lupine and lavender drape down the slope from my porch. Beneath my heart, the tender footstep is there. I close my eyes and it becomes a light pounce.

I never wanted to hurt her. What I wanted was the touch and the holding—of her, by her. I wanted safety, for her and for me. In the hospital, seeing her face so taut and her eyes so dim, and then seeing the change to a face of welcome and eyes that met mine and saw me—I wanted more of that. She allowed me to help her. I wanted to save her. God knows I wanted her to save me.

The hammock holds me with such ease. I bring my left arm up from its dangling and touch the cat-step throb in my solar plexus. Getting older has changed my body from the one I brought to her. My fingers are thickening, rings are harder to get on. My waist also has a thickness now. I'm not fat but my waist has filled out, the taut severity of my youth replaced with a relaxed kind of meat that is, I think, more pleasing to touch than the body of my youth.

I pulled off my sweatshirt and T-shirt and welcomed the cooling of my skin in the air. She was sweating too, her hair wet where I caressed it back from her eyes, cheeks, forehead. She left her hands where they were, together on the bed above her. I climbed on top of her, placed my hands under her shoulders, lowered my chest to hers, and drew my cheek across her face and ear. I tucked my forehead onto the covers alongside her head and let the shape of my body melt into hers.

For a long while we just lay together. He nuzzled his face into my neck and shifted around, resting on his elbows, trying to spare me his full weight. Otherwise he was still.

88

My heart was still beating hard and my breath skipping in tiny gasps in my constricted throat, almost a hiccupping. Another breath—his, smoother and fuller—began to touch mine in a cadence that eased my panting.

There was no thought, but I remember the moment of my choice. I lifted my hands from the pillow above me and brought them down to caress his hair. His shoulders were moving, and their undulation drew me so that I stroked them into rest and stroked down his back over scarring and embedded shrapnel. A cloud of shame darkened my heart, but it swept through immediately. Strangely, I felt proud: I had the right to be there.

I pushed him back and wriggled my shirt up my body and over my head, over my arms and hands. I threw it on the floor. He circled his arms around my chest and took off my bra. Standing up, he kicked off his shoes and pulled his socks off. He took off my pants and underpants, and his own. Then he touched my face, his eyes questioning. I reached up for him. When he lay again on top of me, sensation surged in my groin, and my hips began to reach for him. His responded. I felt my wetness and his hardening. He slipped inside me and began to move so slightly and finely I could not help but gasp, caught between pleasure and the fright still held in my body, until the fear left me in a rush and was replaced by complete ease in surrender.

I think now of myself at age three, on a beach on Ocrakoke, not far from where I now live, wearing a red-striped bathing suit and holding a pail and shovel—alone but under the watchful eye, I am sure, of my mother. I dug sand at that place where waves instantly, faithfully, perpetually fill up your diggings so the hole becomes a shallow puddle of swirling, heavy sludge. I was happy to dig and dig again and dig again and have the warm ocean swoosh against my legs and small, disappearing toes, and have the hole almost but not quite fill up, and my feet feel the sucking and end up sunken further into the shifting, scary sand. Once or twice a vigorous wave came in and knocked me down; I simply started over. I was absorbed in my serious task and would not have welcomed intrusion—even as a child, my aloneness was firmly established—but I knew without thinking that my mother kept watch; I was safe and protected.

That night in Boston, this stranger-lover gave me the ocean and the over-and-over-again waves that kept coming, waves of sweetness and fury, taking and giving. We moved from evening's light entering through the slant of the Venetian blinds to a steady darkness, a moist, soft cave that was stricken through the slats by the soft rays of streetlights and the sharper rays of passing cars. In those hours, our lovemaking was unending: tender and wild, sleepy and harsh. At times he was rough. When he was forceful, I broke through into my own hard craving and my own hard assault. He welcomed it.

But mostly we were kind. One time he was drawing his fingers over my cheekbone, bringing the sculpture of my face into being. I lifted my face to receive more, and a sob burst out of him, sudden tears streaming down his face, his eyes still open and gazing at me. I wiped his tears away and licked their salt from my fingers. We slept then, our skin settling like soft fine dust around the hard lines of our bones.

But once, far into the night, brutality possessed him.

When she lowered her hands to pet and play with the short mane at my nape, I lost the distance between everything. She gave herself to me. I think that is how she held her own. With a hard motion, she pushed me up and tore off her shirt. She lay back again and I reached for her.

Her bra was a trifling pink flow of hardly any cloth, so slight that my fingers barely felt it as I unfastened it and slipped it off. Her nipples were hard, her breasts perfectly small. I saw the breath quickening in her chest and a tremor of pulse in the triangle of white flesh between her ribs. Standing, I unfastened her trousers and slid them off, and her underpants. I kicked off my shoes and took off my jeans and briefs.

Looking up from my hammock now, I see a small cloud forming above the mountains in the silver sky. Exactly as that cloud expands and drifts, that is how the time with her was. We moved according to the whimsy of our bodies and the night around us—the shafts of light, the hot air from the radiator, our hair, fingernails, the moisture and smells of our bodies, and a scent of magnolia in her room. She was naturally kind, and I was kind to her as well. Once, the kindness swept so strongly through my body that I burst into tears.

After I cried, our loving slowed into a light sleep. But I rested too much, and when a truck outside her window gunned its engine and backfired, I struck out, the defense of a soldier, a hard fist to her face. She screamed. Instantly I was back with her, saying, "oh, god, oh, god," and "no, no, no, I didn't mean it." I covered her mouth to stop her screaming and caressed her cheek and jaw where the bone underneath was maybe broken. She struggled, her eyes wide. I kept telling her, "I'm sorry, I didn't mean it, shh, shh." I was truly, truly sorry.

Today, I'm still sorry. I'm so, so sorry to have hit her. It was a brutal blow, a terrible thing. And I'm sorry that I scared her so badly when I first broke in. I wanted to be with her and I didn't know how. I'm sorry for every moment she had of fear.

I'm crying again, feeling not guilt but fierce sorrow.

Amid the abandon, craving, and blood-deep peace that I found with him, all was lost when he struck out and hit me. We were lying on our sides facing each other, half asleep. His leg was bent over mine, our arms crossing each other's breasts and holding each other's shoulders, our other hands folded loosely together between us. We were enclosed in smells and warmth.

Then a loud noise exploded from a truck outside on the street. He convulsed and half rose from the bed and struck my face hard. The pain that pierced my jaw and cheekbone were overshadowed by the terror that swept into me. My chest seized with a raging panic, and my mouth turned cotton dry. I was so helpless, and he was so vicious. I screamed and writhed to get free. He covered my mouth. Immediately he was shushing me, stroking my hair, touching the place he had struck.

He turned on the lamp. He felt me cringe and said, "Rest, rest. It's only light." He stroked my throat and laid his hand on my chest, and suddenly I was sobbing. I turned my face away from the light. I feared another blow, and a burst of panic rose up inside me so violently that I thought I would throw up. But there was no more violence. Gradually, I quieted.

He left the bedroom for a few minutes and returned with ice cubes wrapped in a kitchen towel. He held it to my jaw. Under the freezing remedy my face felt better, and I fell asleep. I think I slept for a long time. I woke up feeling impossibly peaceful.

When I opened my eyes, he was sitting beside me with his eyes closed, stroking the quilt on my bed. It was a quilt my mother made for me when I was eighteen. It's a beautiful quilt, but a girl just gone away to college doesn't know a quilt as intimately as a child does. So the quilt on the bed was not as precious to me as my other one, hidden away for safekeeping in my closet.

That one, my childhood quilt, is made of twelve patches, each with the same pattern of butterflies and flowers, sewn with leftover scraps of fifteen or twenty different fabrics. The same fabrics appear over and over but in different arrangements so that every patch is unique, and no two flowers or butterflies are alike. I loved certain of the fabrics more than others, tending to adore most the palest ones with the tiniest, most subtle designs. My mother did not make bright-colored clothing. In the years of my childhood, I lay on the quilt and stroked this butterfly or that flower or traced with my finger this or that line of stitches outlining the figures or joining the patches. I wore it out with my devotion, and now it was fragile, protected in plastic in the closet.

He was touching the quilt on the bed in the same way. I gently bit my lip to stop the tears that welled in me. Before that, even when I had yielded and joined him sexually, I was holding out against him somewhere inside myself. Then when he struck me it seemed that all my trust was idiocy. How was it, then, that I gave in to him so completely that I showed him my childhood quilt? It was the kinship with him. "The wrong quilt," I murmured. "It's in the closet."

His finger stopped moving, and I watched his chest rise and fall with a long breath. "Show me," he said.

If I follow that cat-step in my belly now, it leads me to the way her leg stretched so the pale foot could reach the floor beside the bed. I let her go, and she moved in her freedom just as she moved while under me. She was liquid with love by then and could not help but move as if she were a cloud or a dream.

Her step was silent on the thick carpet. Her hand was light on the closet doorknob, and the door clicked smoothly open. I thought there might be a weapon and stood up to stand close behind her.

She paid no attention to me, lifted out her special quilt folded up in a plastic bag, and moved to the bed. She took the quilt out and opened it partway, then shivered even though the room was so hot.

I knew what to do. I eased her backward to lie on the bed, leaning back on the pillows. Then, as carefully as she handled it, I picked up the quilt and opened it and placed it over her, arranging the butterflies and flowers that were so ragtag, some flapping loose at the edges. "Rest now," I told her. She closed her eyes.

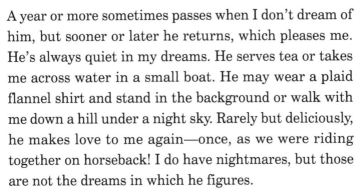

A year or more sometimes passes when I don't dream of him, but sooner or later he returns, which pleases me. He's always quiet in my dreams. He serves tea or takes me across water in a small boat. He may wear a plaid flannel shirt and stand in the background or walk with me down a hill under a night sky. Rarely but deliciously, he makes love to me again—once, as we were riding together on horseback! I do have nightmares, but those are not the dreams in which he figures.

Dreaming and awakening sometimes interact. Sometimes you wake from a happy dream and wish to go back to the delights you had in your sleep. Sometimes it's the opposite, awakening and being afraid to go back to sleep for fear of the horrors in the dream. Sometimes, too, it is waking life that holds some particularly devastating event, and you wake up feeling normal but very quickly remember the dreadful thing that is happening in your life. This happened to me when my brother died, and again when I got very sick and every day was a terrible struggle, and I did not know how I could complete my internship. When you wake up from sleep as if all were well, and then quickly the waking truth of loss or danger comes upon you, it paralyzes you with dread or sorrow.

That was happening to me in the weeks before I met him. Three or four times, I had a dream of walking out of the ICU, never to return, walking down the street into a bright field of flowers. And then I would wake to realize I must go back to the hospital that day. It made me cry.

He entered my dreams before the night with him was even finished. After I got my quilt from the closet, he laid it over me and I slept for a while, and I dreamt of him sweetly touching me. When I awoke, there was a moment of longing for the dissolving touch of the dream, and then I remembered where I was and what was happening. Thrown into profound distress that he might have gone, I spun around to look for him, saw him sitting at the foot of the bed looking at me, and fell into shaking. I was truly afraid then—not of him but of myself. I was terrified at my longing for this stranger.

She was so wise. The cover she got out of the closet gave me such a fine way to leave her. I caressed each butterfly, every flower, for they were all different, and once I started it seemed wrong to leave any of them out. It quieted me. As I touched the flowers and the butterflies, the pure soft cotton beauty of her quilt, I knew I was saying goodbye.

For so many years, I have pushed away the memory of her. I thought that was because I couldn't face the badness of what I did. But right now, I wonder if the worst thing I did that day was to leave her. I could not have stayed; I was not a person then who could have any kind of relationship. I could not even have a conversation. But now I mourn. I wish that what we had might have been cherished and allowed to grow.

Instead, I left. I knew where I needed to go, and it was less than a week later that I walked the dust of the desert. I have continued coming home ever since.

This morning the creeping cat has allowed me to step further into the memory than ever, and my wanting to know the goodness has been fulfilled. I look up and see the mountains. What I did with her is just as impossible as the existence of the mountains, and it was no more evil than they are. Today I've found out that I have been pushing away not badness but so much good, true life.

I would like to sleep now; the dry heat is making me tired. I'm not old, but lately the soles of my feet ache when I walk. Even so, later today I want to go all the way out to the mailbox and back, stepping like the cats so I can know what their life is like and to gain for myself the knowledge that they have, and to thank the cat-stepping for the understanding it brought me today.

He was touching butterflies and flowers, pondering over them the way I used to. He seemed drowsy, as I was. I felt I could lie forever under my quilt with him visiting each square, stroking the threads and fabrics with thumb and forefinger.

The traffic increased outside, and gray daylight appeared. I slept again, and when I woke, he was putting on his clothes—jeans, sweatshirt, socks, sneakers. I began shaking and he petted me in long strokes all down my body, over the quilt, quieting me. When he let himself out of the apartment, I felt as helpless as when he first broke in. I huddled dazed beneath the quilt, in and out of sleep, whimpering. When I got up, I washed, with severe regret, and there was no question of telling anyone. I never did.

I never even told myself the whole truth until today. Over all the years, that event has waited for me to look at it. Before I have only glanced. Sometimes, flippant and crass, I have told myself that the weary, cynical doctor I was then just needed a good fuck. Always I have judged that I betrayed myself. I could have fought harder or told him to leave, called the police. But those are small, partial truths. Those are really not truths at all, but deceptions. Today I believe that a greater betrayal happened when I said nothing to keep him from leaving. But I also know that was impossible.

Sometimes, remembering the power and depth and joy, I have judged that I must be denying reality by giving false meaning and beauty to our meeting. He attacked me. The violation was a shock my body will never forget. But things are often not what they are labeled. He did assault and traumatize me, and that is not all he did.

Today, I cherish the gift. To look truthfully at some-one and to allow him or her to see you as well—this is essential healing. To allow yourself to give and receive the care so badly needed, this is solace. This is cure.

It was Wednesday. I spent the day in fugue states, half-sleep. On Thursday I tidied the apartment and went out to do chores. On Friday I walked the blankets of gold and red leaves on the sidewalks, ate a large meal at a deli. Saturday, I dressed and put makeup on the bruise on my face. I left early and arrived at the hospital settled and eager. When I walked into the ICU that day, I felt again the ghost of Jimmy's breathless throat under my fingers. It aroused in me not fear or distress, but a soft caring.

Today, with the same tenderness, I remember the gaze exchanged yesterday with Violet. But just as the body remembers healing, it never erases trauma. I lift my hand up and touch my jaw, soothing the fear that has stayed lodged there for forty years. It is an old friend. Staying here as it does, always returning, it gives me the chance over and over to ease my pain.

Morning is well underway. The dawn clouds have flown high, and sunlight is casting strong shadows on the drifts of sand and giving bright tips to the waves. I'm going to go for a swim. I'll walk down the sand, then dive and swim out, turning onto my back to let the saltwater hold me on the heave and chop of its motion. I'll feel the surprises of lift, sideways pull, the patches of cold. I'll know of the secret unknowns below. I'll swim back in and lie on the warming sand with the waves hissing and birds crying. Then I'll walk home, shower, and put on music: Vivaldi, or Annie Lennox. I'll make cupcakes, chocolate with lemon frosting, to bring with me this afternoon. Some friends have invited me for coffee. They'll be surprised when I tell them it's my birthday.

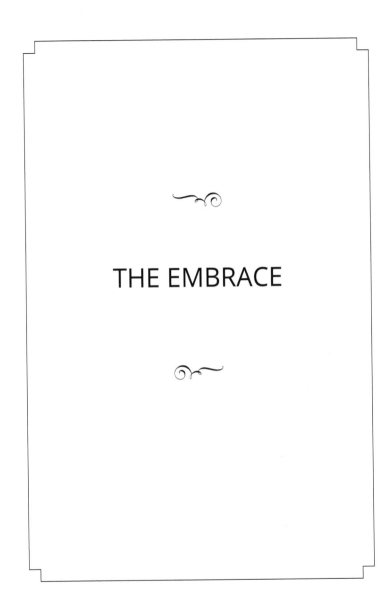

THE EMBRACE

There is a picture I hold in my mind: a black devil man with six arms and a big grin and little white skulls circling his head, coupling with a six-armed lady sitting on his lap. The picture is small, framed in black wood. It used to sit on top of a sloppy stack of books crammed on the edge of a windowsill next to your television. For years I hardly noticed it.

Then, for a minute or two, I owned it. "That's you," you said with utter conviction, poking your head toward the corner of the room. "That's *you*." You lurched out of your recliner, a hulking ludicrous obese Rasputin wearing a dark purple velour bathrobe and dirty white running shoes. Fetching the little dark picture from its inconsequential display, you offered it to me. "Here, you should have this. I want to give this to you."

I came close, to accept your gift. For nine years you had been my supervisor and consultant in my work as a therapist; more truthfully, you had been my teacher in the art of living well. Through all that time, the only gifts exchanged were intangibles: attentiveness, friendliness, open minds, and impactful words. We never touched, but a complicated attraction was always present. We acted like magnets whose two ends constantly swiveled. Just when we were immutably sucking toward each other, one of us, and then immediately the other, would turn around and force ourselves apart. You once said to me with your inimitable bluntness: "You don't know whether you want to fuck me or kill me." I believe the same was true for you.

But in these days of your sickness, something different had at last been allowed. You reached out as if *you* had six arms and were trying to use them all to claim your life and wanted me to help. It was hard to stay close to you, though, because most of the time, the arms swung about in fear and fury, fighting uselessly with each other or grasping for different things all at once. You flailed endlessly in crazed campaigns against everyone who had ever hurt you, plus anyone you thought might. You asked for me, then told me I said all the wrong things and accused me of wanting to kill you. You wouldn't answer my calls, or you said you didn't want to see me.

But by then I had lots of arms too, and I was relentless. Even when you used all six to push me away, I never stopped coming back. Every time I did, your arms opened up again—in true welcome and simple need. Reaching, beckoning, and holding, our miraculous new growth of arms and hands displayed an immense, essential sanity that could heal us both or even all of us in the world.

And now yours offered a gift. I looked at the picture

you held out to me. The two demons were entwined as if there could be no higher purpose on Earth or in Heaven. Arms and eyes were everywhere. The two wore shameless smiles—hers blissful, his triumphant. The picture's darkness was stunning. These two dwelled in a place like the center of the Earth.

I laid it carefully on my jacket and bag by the door, to carry out to my car. "Wait!" you called. "Give me that picture." I did, and you held it close to your face and hung over it, wavering as you stood in the hall in your bathrobe. "Put it back," you ordered, handing it over and pointing toward the corner of the room, climbing again into your chair. I set the picture down where it had been.

You watched it, held your hands out to me. "You can't take it with you now. I'm sorry. I'm having a hard time that you're leaving. I can't give it to you now. I can see it from here. It will remind me of you. Is that okay? I want to be able to look at it. You can't take it now. Later."

"That's fine," I said. I sat on the chair's edge, grateful to feel your warm leg next to mine and your warm, dry hands in mine.

For weeks after that, sitting beside you as you slept, I sometimes thought of taking the picture. The room, and your whole house, was like a feast: every table, shelf, mantel, wall, sill, and much of the floor were covered with paintings, photographs, etchings, drawings, weavings, stones, sculptures, pieces of wood, metal, fabric, talismans. The dark little picture of the many-armed lovers was surely not a thing anyone else even knew was there. I could take it, and no one would be bothered.

But then I would think, maybe someone *does* know it's there: your son, your sister. They would miss it, and they would know I had taken it. They might even come into the room just at the wrong moment, and instead of finding me sitting next to you, I would be hunched over in the corner stuffing something into my bag. Or *you* would see me do it, watching through your apparently closed eyes as I squirreled it away.

Now you're gone, and I'd like to have it. But if I ask for it, it's a silly mess. I'd have to tell some story—maybe the truth, something like the truth, briefly—and your son would have to make a decision. I imagine myself saying: "He gave me that picture, but he wanted to keep it for a while." It sounds lame, but it's not a fifteenth-century Ming vase I'm asking for.

Or I might say, "That picture represents our work together. It's the place where Tibetan Buddhism meets Jung—a coniunctio." Technically correct, but words like that are way too far from the real truth.

How about this: "We talked about that picture one day while I was there, and he said he'd like me to have it." Not bad. I could live with that.

~⸿

What is really true? People don't have six arms. If they did, things would be different. We might then live in a world where the dreams I've dreamed mean something. Since instead we live in this well-ordered, two-armed world, my dreams probably mean nothing. Unfortunately, you and I believe otherwise, which makes us crazy. You and I have to take everything we know into account, including our dreams, bodies, visions.

When I first heard you had a brain tumor, I dropped immediately into a wide and deep river of gold that carried you kindly and was not dependent on medical science or my ability to wish you into wellness. When panic and sadness would consume me, over the months, I sometimes found it possible to fall into that stream; it seemed always available, though sometimes deeper than I was able to dive. I believed it would help you.

Sleeping, I also found love. I was grateful for a sweet,

healing dream of kissing the left side of your head where the surgical scar jagged over your bald contours. Another night gave me this wonder: a shimmering gold fish is eaten by a dull-eyed black fish, which then excretes the remains of the gold one to lie forever on the ocean floor, and the whole experience is held by a luminous ocean of morning-glory blue. Two-armed people would view that one dubiously, but to me it was supremely comforting. I told it to you, and your smile said everything.

But unlovely things also crept out of me during the night. In one dream, I pitied you and said, "I'm glad *I* don't have a brain tumor." Even my waking hours were laced with petty, evil thoughts. Helping you, I felt saintly. Mentioning my sick friend to other people allowed me to feel special. Hearing you talk of your terror one time unloosed a stirring of sadistic satisfaction in me. Disgusted at the ugliness of it, I was driven to write down in a very private place the demons that were swarming out of me, in hopes of containing them:

I love it that he's got a brain tumor!
I love him having his brains totally scrambled.
I love him being helpless, vulnerable.
I love him being the crazy one.
I love the creeping black poisons in his skull.

I would love to do it to him myself: gnash gnaw tear and chew away at his brain!

Frightened of myself by then, I ended the page with this ragged hope:

I'm spent. I thought there would be more, maybe it will come to me.

Maybe it's enough for now. God forgive me.

Writing takes the darkness upon itself. The paper swallowed the poison and left me free of it. I knew that the two crazed lovers came together in the foul places as much as in the bright.

⁓

You lived only five months from diagnosis to death. At first, I visited every few days. You liked to go for drives, always thanked me and gave me money for gas. Once you directed me to a farm far out in West County. I stayed in the car while you staggered to the yard and talked to a man. When you came back, you said, "Ordered firewood for the winter." On another ride we drove to a Catholic monastery the next county over. I waited in the car while you went into the chapel.

After a while, walking to and from the car was no

longer possible for you. In the house, you were settled into the living room in a recliner. One day you asked me to go upstairs into your bedroom and bring something to you. "Second drawer, under socks." I went upstairs. Unlike the living room, your bedroom was orderly and had few things in it. The second dresser drawer opened smoothly; there were the socks, balled up cottons and wools, grey and white and argyle and brown. I fished around and felt a large metal object, which I drew out. Heavy. Black and steel.

I am not a gun person. I held it in both hands like a large, fragile egg or a bomb that might go off. Shook my head and sighed. Closed the drawer and carried the gun downstairs.

You smiled when the gun and I appeared. You gestured toward a back room. "Put it in there? Behind the picture leaning against the chair." It was a framed Van Gogh print, crows flying over a field of wheat. "Just on the floor there, behind."

That afternoon your son, a serious young man leaning toward obesity, arrived and went directly upstairs. He came down immediately and motioned me to join him in the hallway. "Something is missing."

I looked at him.

"There was a gun upstairs."

"He asked me to move it."

"Where?"

"The back room. Behind the Van Gogh print."

He grimaced. "Of course."

I said a quick goodbye to you and left for the day.

Not long after, you stopped talking and slept most of every day. They moved you to a hospital bed in the living room. A nurse was there during the day, and a few of us took turns staying with you overnight, sleeping on the couch in your consulting room where each of us had sat for years. The nights were quiet.

Your last conscious day, I sat beside you. When you saw me come in, after days of absence, a fast boundless joy crossed your face exactly like a little act of nature—a small bird zinging by, a silver rippling in water, a falling star.

The day was bad after that. You had long since lost the power of speech, and I found mine was gone too. No kind words, no reassurance, no stories or dreams did I tell you. I sat mute beside you as you continually reached for the bed rail with your one still usable arm and pulled yourself as if to get out, and then fell back. It was an hour or more after you kept fingering your shirt that I figured out you might want it to be unbuttoned and did that for you. All day you seemed to be burning inside, and we had nothing for each other but an occasional strong meeting of our eyes, mutually helpless. I left quickly that day after the nurse administered morphine against your enfeebled, wordless protest. I held your arm for the injection, and you looked at me as if I didn't understand.

Stepping outside your house and walking across the grass to my car, I marveled that my feet made their way so thoughtlessly, that two such small feet held all my weight, that I moved where I wanted to and didn't fall over or sink into a heap. The air, unimaginably fresh, moved without thought in and out of my nostrils, giving me life. The same air pushed itself down into my chest and found a demon coiled there, stricken with guilt and sorrow.

During that night, the six-armed people came and spent the entire night with me. Visions are not just visual; they take place within our bodies. That night I was consumed.

When I got back to you in the morning, a priest was

leaving after working his odd mysteries. You were still alive but different: motionless, one arm outside the covers, cold, the hand clenched. Your eyes were unmoving in a gaze that searched upward. I was finally able to talk, and when no one else was in the room I told you some things I thought you might need to know, as well as some other things I just wanted you to know.

Yesterday I finally asked your son for the picture. He remembered it, and he promised it would be mine when he sorts out your things. He was generous and willing, and I was grateful for his easy agreement. But I know your son has the troubled mixtures of your blood washing through his veins, so it won't surprise me if I never actually get it.

And it truly doesn't matter now. The picture is embedded in my memory. Memories are not frozen records of the past; they are living in the present, throbbing and radiating throughout our bodies. The dark picture dwells in my solar plexus, in the soles of my feet, all along my spine, and in the palms of my hands. I hear the moans and gasps of the twelve-armed couple. I taste the salt of their skin and tears, and the sweet, rare flavor of their blood. Their smells are sour, then vanilla and smoky. The pressures and heats of their clasping sweep through me, head to toe, then toe to head. I see their undulating blackness, their redness, and their goldness with eyes that look within myself, millions of eyes within.

ACKNOWLEDGMENTS

First, thanks to dear friends for unimaginable loyalty in trusting that this book deserved to happen and for a lot of laughter and understanding: Barry Leibman, Helen Cooluris, Nell Kneibler, Catherine Sharp, and Maria Monroe.

Thanks to my writers' group of twenty years for steadfastly listening to these stories, offering new ways of seeing them, and inspiring me by sharing their own fine writing: Marko Fong, Linda Saldaña, Richard Gustafson, Sarah Amador, Nick Valdez, Nancy Bourne, and others come and gone over the years. Special thanks to writing group colleague Jo-Anne Rosen, for her generosity in helping me publish and for being an excellent model of integrity and devotion to writing and to other people.

Thanks to other dear friends who've believed and inspired over many years: Arlene Bernstein, Judith Kay Nelson, Mimi Wolfe, Mary Killian, and Jan Lowry-Cole.

Thanks to Michael Rex at Russian River Books and Letters in Guerneville, California, for having such a fine fiction collection and being happy to add this book to it, and for his energetic support for writing in our small community. Thanks to others in that local community for their appreciation and example, especially Dan Coshnear.

Thanks to Reedsy.com for their array of resources and webinars in support of indie writers. Thanks very especially to Margaret Diehl for guiding me into the depths of my stories and for the wisdom of her editing. Thanks to Ellen Tarlin for her fine eye and sense in copy editing and proofreading. Thanks to Asya Blue for carrying the book patiently and expertly into its visual glory with design.

Thanks to Thomas Pope and Jack Kornfield for encouraging me with their appreciation for my stories, and for their teachings on how to be happy.

Thanks to all friends, clients, and strangers who have given their presence to these stories.

Thanks to my sister, Joan Johnson, for always, always, being there.

Thanks to my husband, Doug Wheatley, for helping keep my feet on the ground and my heart in the light, through wounding and healing.

ABOUT THE AUTHOR

Judith Day is a psychotherapist in Sonoma County, California. Born and raised in St. Louis, Missouri, she has written fiction since childhood. Her stories have appeared in *Persimmon Tree*, *Canyon Voices*, *Buffalo Almanack*, and other journals. She has been a cook and a cab driver, and she has graduate degrees in history and psychology.

In private practice since receiving her master's degree in counseling from the California Institute of Integral Studies in 1985, she has also worked in emergency psychiatric response, inpatient psychiatric settings, residential treatment, low-fee mental health clinics, and as a military family life consultant. Since 1993 she has taught mindfulness meditation.

This is her first book. A second collection of stories is scheduled to be published in 2024.

She has been married forty years and lives with her husband near the ocean in northern California. She may be contacted at books@judithday.com.